AF271407

VECTOR
CALCULUS

MAVEN BOOKS

VECTOR CALCULUS

DURGAPRASANNA BHATTACHARYYA, M.A.

Professor of Mathematics, Barielly College, U.P.

MAVEN BOOKS

Chennai   Trichy   Tirunelveli   New Delhi

Honour Copyright
&
Exclude Piracy

This book is protected by copyright. Reproduction of any part in any form including photocopying shall not be done except with authorization from the publisher.

MAVEN BOOKS

An Imprint of **MJP Publishers**

ISBN 978-93-88191-15-9 **MAVEN Books**

All rights reserved No. 44, Nallathambi Street,
Printed and bound in India Triplicane, Chennai 600 005

MJP 589 © Publishers, 2019

Publisher : **C. Janarthanan**

This book is a reproduction of an important historical work. MAVEN Books uses state-of-the-art technology to digitally reconstruct the work, preserving the original format whilst repairing imperfections present in the aged copy. In rare cases, an imperfection in the original, such as a blemish or missing page, may be replicated in our edition. We do, however, repair the vast majority of imperfections successfully; any imperfections that remain are intentionally left to preserve the state of such historical works.

PUBLISHER'S NOTE

The legacy of a country is in its varied cultural heritage, historical literature, developments in the field of economy and science. The top nations in the world are competing in the field of science, economy and literature. This vast legacy has to be conserved and documented so that it can be bestowed to the future generation. The knowledge of this legacy is slowly getting perished in the present generation due to lack of documentation.

Keeping this in mind, the concern with retrospective acquiring of rare books has been accented recently by the burgeoning reprint industry. MAVEN Books is gratified to retrieve the rare collections with a view to bring back those books that were landmarks in their time.

In this effort, a series of rare books would be republished under the banner, "MAVEN Books". The books in the reprint series have been carefully selected for their contemporary usefulness as well as their historical importance within the intellectual. We reconstruct the book with slight enhancements made for better presentation, without affecting the contents of the original edition.

Most of the works selected for republishing covers a huge range of subjects, from history to anthropology. We believe this reprint edition will be a service to the numerous researchers and practitioners active in this fascinating field. We allow readers to experience the wonder of peering into a scholarly work of the highest order and seminal significance.

MAVEN Books

CONTENTS

VECTOR CALCULUS

INTRODUCTION

In course of an attempt to apply direct vector methods to certain problems of Electricity and Hydrodynamics, it was felt that, at least as a matter of consistency, the foundations of Vector Analysis ought to be placed on a basis independent of any reference to cartesian coordinates and the main theorems of that Analysis established directly from first principles. The result of my work in .this connection is embodied in the present paper and an attempt is made here to develop the Differential and Integral Calculus of Vectors from a point of view which is believed to be new.

In order to realise the special features of my presentation of the subject, it will be convenient to recall briefly the usual method of treatment. In any vector problem we are given certain relations among a number of vectors and we have to deduce some other relations which these same vectors satisfy. Now what we do in the usual method is to resolve each vector into three arbitrary components and thus rob it first entirely of its vectorial character. The various characteristic vector operators like the gradient and curl are also subjected to the same process of dissection. We then work the whole problem out with our familiar scalar calculus, and when the necessary analysis has been completed, we collect our components and read the result in vector language. It is of course quite useful so far as it goes, the final vector expression of the result giving not only a succinct look to our formulæ but also a suggestiveness of interpretation which they had been lacking in their bulky cartesian forms. But surely, strictly speaking, we should not call it Vector Analysis at all, but only Cartesian Analysis in vector language. In Vector Analysis proper we have, or ought to have, the vector physical magnitudes which our vectors represent, direct before our minds, and this characteristic advantage of being in direct close touch with the only relevant elements of our problem is sacrificed straight away, if we throw over our vectors at the very outset and work with cartesian components. We sacrifice in fact the very soul of Vector Analysis and what remains amounts practically to a system of abridged notation for certain complicated formulæ and operators of cartesian calculus which happen to recur every now and then in physical applications.

The one great fact in favour of this plan is that it affords us greater facility for working purposes, this facility no doubt arising solely from our previous exclusive familiarity with Cartesian Analysis. But however useful it might be in this direction, and generally in making the existing body of Cartesian Analysis available for vector purposes, the process, I venture to think, is at best transitional, and the importance of the subject and the importance of our thinking of vector physical magnitudes direct as vectors, alike seem to demand that the whole of this branch of Analysis should be placed on an independent basis.

But there is a peculiar difficulty at the very outset. Historically, most of the characteristic concepts of Vector Analysis, like the divergence and curl, had been arrived at by the physicist and the mathematician in course of their work with the Cartesian calculus and had even become quite familiar before the possibility of Vector Analysis as a distinct branch of mathematics by itself was explicitly recognised. The vector analyst at first then starts from these old concepts which happen also to be the most fundamental, but it is his object right from the beginning to exhibit them no longer in their cartesian forms, but in terms of the characteristic physical or geometrical attributes which they stand for. Very often now a question of selection arises from among the number of ways in which the same concept may be defined, different definitions being framed according to the different points of view from which the subject is intended to be developed. The physicist—who, by the way, makes the greatest practical use of Vector Analysis and whose sole interest also in the subject is determined by the service it renders him in his work—aims, first of all, at his definition representing most directly a familiar physical fact or idea; but, at the same time, and very naturally too, he holds the possibility of the definition yielding quite easily his useful working formulæ, of equally vital importance. But, unfortunately enough, these two distinct aims of the physicist are irreconcileable with each other, the most natural definition from the physical point of view leads to the useful transformation formulæ of Physics only with the greatest difficulty, and the definition that yields these formulae with any facility is generally hopelessly artificial from the physical point of view.* It is this irreconcileability of the two distinct purposes of the physicist which, I venture to suppose, is directly responsible for the persistence of cartesian calculus in Vector Analysis. For what is done is that definitions are first framed with a view to direct summing up of the simplest appropriate physical ideas, but then the necessity almost inevitably arises of seeking cartesian expressions for working purposes, for making Vector Analysis a serviceable and at the same time an easily manageable tool in the hands of the physicist.

I may just illustrate my point by recalling how the usual definitions of the two most characteristic concepts of Vector

---

* Reference may be made here to a paper by Mr. E. B. Wilson in the *Bulletin of the American Math. Soc.*, vol. 16, on Unification of Vectorial Notations, where he criticises the artificiality in the definitions of divergence and curl by an Italian mathematician, Burali Forti, which were chosen solely with a view to their adaptability for establishing the working formulæ of Vector Analysis with ease. Thus Burali Forti's definition of divergence is div $V = a$. [grad $(a. v) + $ curl $(a \times v)$], where a is any constant unit vector. This has certainly no direct connection with any intrinsic property of the divergence, physical or otherwise.

Analysis have been adopted from 'the simplest physical ideas which immediately identify them. Thus the idea of divergence is taken directly from Hydrodynamics, and keeping before our minds the picture of fluid leaving (or entering) a small closed space, we define the divergence of a vector function at a point as the limit of the ratio, if one exists, of the surface-integral * of the function over a small closed space surrounding the point to the volume enclosed by the surface, a unique limit being supposed to be reached by the closed surface shrinking up' to a point in any manner.

Again, it is found that some vector fields can be specified completely by the gradient of a scalar function, so that the line integral † of the vector function along any closed curve in (simply connected) space would vanish. Thus the work done is nil along any closed path in a conservative field of force. But, in case the vector function cannot be so specified, an expression of this negative quality of the function at a point is naturally sought in its now non-evanescent line integral along a small closed (plane) path surrounding the point. The ratio of this line integral to the area enclosed by our path generally approaches a limit as the path shrinks up to a point, independently of its original form and of the manner of its shrinking, but depending on the orientation of its plane. The limit moreover has usually a maximum value, subject to the variation of this orientation, and a vector of magnitude equal to this maximum value and drawn perpendicular to that aspect of the plane which gives us the maximum value is called the curl of the original vector function.

Now these definitions, embodying, as they do, the most essential physical attributes of divergence and curl, must be regarded as perhaps the most appropriate ones that could be given from the physicist's point of view. But then comes the

---

* By the surface integral of a vector function, we always mean the surface integral of its normal component.

† By the line integral of a vector function, we always mean the line integral of its tangential component.

practical problem of deducing from these definitions the working rules of manipulation of these operators. The direct deduction being extremely difficult,* the already acquired facility in working cartesian calculus is naturally utilised for the purpose, and thus is reached the present position of Vector Analysis which I have already described.

The only way out of the dilemma would seem to be found by ignoring altogether both of these two specific interests of the physicist and looking straight, without any bias, to the requirements of Vector Analysis as a branch of Pure Mathematics by itself. And paradoxical though it may sound, this course perhaps would ultimately best serve the physicist's ends also. At any rate, no free development of any science is certainly possible, so long as we require it at every step to serve some narrow specific end.

We ask ourselves then, what should be the most natural starting point of the Differential Calculus of Vectors? All our old familiar ideas of differential calculus suggest at once that, whatever the ultimately fundamental concepts might be, we should begin by an examination of the relation between the differential of the vector function (of the position of a point P in space) corresponding to a small displacement of the point P and this displacement. This very straightforward line of enquiry I propose to conduct here, and it will be seen how in a very natural sense we can look upon the divergence and curl as really the fundamental concepts of the Differential Calculus of vectors, and how this new point of view materially simplifies our analysis.

The first three sections are preliminary. In the first two I summarise the definitions of continuous functions and of Integrals and briefly touch upon just those properties which I require in course of my work. The third is devoted to the Gradient of a scalar function. The real thesis of the paper I

---

* Compare, for instance, the difficulty encountered by Mr. E. Cunningham in a paper on the Theory of Functions of a Real Vector in the *Proceedings of the Lond. Math. Soc.*, vol. 12, 1913.

begin in the fourth section where I consider the Linear Vector Function only with a view to developing what I have called the scalar and vector constants of the linear function, and although there is nothing very special about these ideas themselves, they will be found to lead very naturally to the concepts of Divergence and Curl and have been made here the foundation on which my Differential Calculus is built. The fifth section is devoted to that Differential Calculus and in the sixth I consider a few Integration Theorems and the divergence and curl of an integral with a view to showing with what ease these operations can be performed from my point of view.

Notation.

With regard to notation I use Gibbs' here, although some of its features are obviously meant to suggest easy ways of passing from Cartesian formulæ to vector, and *vice versâ*, with which of course I am not at all concerned.

For convenience of reference I reproduce the notation for the multiplication of vectors.

If A, B are any two vectors,

the *scalar product* of A, B is A.B $=$ | A | | B | cos θ, and the *vector product* is A × B which is a vector of magnitude | A | | B | sin θ, and in direction perpendicular to both A and B; | A |, | B | denoting the tensors of A and B and θ the angle between them.

Again, if A, B, C are any three vectors, the notation [ABC] is used for any one of the three equal products

A.B × C $=$ B.C × A $=$ C.A × B $=$ the volume of the parallelopiped which has A, B, C, for conterminous edges.

The following useful formula will occur very often :

A × (B × C) $=$ (A.C)B $-$ (A.B)C.

I.

CONTINUITY : DIFFERENTIATION OF A VECTOR
FUNCTION OF A SCALAR VARIABLE.

1. The functions we deal with will be mostly continuous. The position of a point P in space being specified as usual by the vector $r(=\overline{OP})$ drawn from a fixed origin O, the function $f(r)$ is said to be continuous at P, if corresponding to every arbitrarily chosen positive number δ, a positive number η (dependent on δ) can be found such that $|f(r+\epsilon)-f(r)| < \delta$, ϵ being any vector satisfying the inequality $|\epsilon| < \eta$. The notation $|V|$ denotes the absolute value of the scalar if V is a scalar, and the tensor of V if V is a vector.

If we construct the vector diagram as well, that is, if by taking another fixed point O' we draw the vector $O'P'$ representing the value of the vector function corresponding to every point P in the region in which the function is defined, then Q being a point in the neighbourhood of P and Q' the corresponding point in the vector diagram, our definition of continuity implies that any positive number δ being first assigned, a positive number η can be found such that so long as the tensor of the vector PQ is less than η, the tensor of $P'Q'$ will be less than δ. It implies in other words that a sphere (of radius η) can be described with centre P such that points Q' in the vector diagram corresponding to all points Q within (not on) this sphere will lie within a sphere of any arbitrarily small radius δ described with centre P'.

We prove now that in the same case the angle $P'O'Q'$, that is, the change in direction suffered by the vector function can also be made arbitrarily small. For, in the triangle $O'P'Q'$,

$$\frac{\sin \mathrm{P'}\overset{\wedge}{\mathrm{O}}\mathrm{'Q'}}{\mathrm{P'Q'}} = \frac{\sin \mathrm{P'}\overset{\wedge}{\mathrm{Q}}\mathrm{'O'}}{\mathrm{O'P'}} \not\times \frac{1}{\mathrm{O'P'}}$$

Hence, $\sin \mathrm{P'}\overset{\wedge}{\mathrm{O}}\mathrm{'Q'} \not\times \dfrac{\mathrm{P'Q'}}{\mathrm{O'P'}}$.

But P'Q' can be made arbitrarily small, and O'P' is supposed to be finite. Hence sin P'O'Q' and therefore also the angle P'O'Q' can be made arbitrarily small. It follows that our continuous vector functions are continuous in direction as well.

2. The function $f(r)$ is said to have a limit at P, if Q being any point in the neighbourhood of P we have the same limiting value of the function no matter in what manner Q approaches P continuously.

If the function is continuous at P, the limit exists at P and is equal to the value of the function at P, and conversely.

If the limit does not exist at P, then either of two things may happen : (i) there may be different limiting values for different approaches to P ; or (ii) there may be no definite limiting value for any approach or some approaches. In either case the function is discontinuous at P.

A third kind of discontinuity arises when the limit exists at P, but this limit is not equal to the value of the function at P.

But, as has been remarked already, we shall concern ourselves practically with continuous functions alone, and an examination of the sort of peculiarities we have just noticed, of what has been described as the Pathology of Functions would be out of place here. The only discontinuity we shall come across is the infinite discontinuity which arises when $|f(r)|$ tends to infinity at P.

3. Turning our attention then to continuous functions alone, we note that the sum and the scalar and vector products of two continuous vector functions are continuous also. The case of sum is almost self evident, and we prove now that if V_1, V_2 are two continuous vector functions, the scalar product $V_1 \cdot V_2$ is continuous.

Let V'_1, V'_2 denote the values of the functions at a point $r+\epsilon$ in the neighbourhood of the point r. We have only to show that for any positive number δ assigned in advance, a positive number η can be found such that

$$| V'_1 \cdot V'_2 - V_1 \cdot V_2 | < \delta,$$

for all vectors ϵ satisfying $| \epsilon | < \eta$.

Now $V'_1 \cdot V'_2 - V_1 \cdot V_2 = [V_1 + (V'_1 - V_1)] \cdot [V_2$

$$+ (V'_2 - V_2)] - V_1 \cdot V_2 = V_1 \cdot (V_2' - V_2)$$
$$+ V_2 \cdot (V_1' - V_1) + (V_1' - V_1) \cdot (V_2' - V_2),$$

which is not greater than $| V_1 | \; | V_2' - V_2 | + | V_2 | \; | V_1' - V_1 | + | V_1' - V_1 | \; | V_2' - V_2 |$, since the magnitude of the scalar product of two vectors is not greater than the product of their tensors.

Hence, since the absolute magnitude of the sum of any number of quantities is not greater than the sum of their absolute magnitudes, we have

$$| V_1' \cdot V_2' - V_1 \cdot V_2 | \not> | V_1 | \; | V_2' - V_2 |$$
$$+ | V_2 | \; | V_1' - V_1 | + | V_1' - V_1 | \; | V_2' - V_2 |$$

But since V_1, V_2 are continuous,

$| V_1' - V_1 | <$ any arbitrary δ_1, provided only $| \epsilon | <$ the corresponding η_1, and $| V_2' - V_2 | < \dots\dots\dots\dots\delta_2 , \dots\dots\dots\dots\eta_2$

Of the two numbers $\eta_1 \; \eta_2$, let $\eta_1 \not> \eta_2$; then provided $| \epsilon | < \eta_1$, $| V_1' - V_1 | < \delta_1$ and $| V_2' - V_2 | < \delta_2$, and therefore $| V_1' \cdot V_2' - V_1 \cdot V_2 | < | V_1 | \delta_2 + | V_2 | \delta_1 + \delta_1 \delta_2$.

Again, since $| V_1 |$, $| V_2 |$ are supposed to be finite, given any positive number δ, we can always find δ_1 and δ_2 such that $\delta > | V_1 | \delta_2 + | V_2 | \delta_1 + \delta_1 \delta_2$.

Choosing such values now of δ_1 and δ_2, we have

$$| V'_1 \cdot V'_2 - 'V_1 \cdot V_2 | < \delta, \text{ whenever } | \epsilon | < \eta_1,$$

which proves our theorem.

Similarly we prove that $V_1 \times V_2$ is also continuous.

2

4. If we consider in particular the continuous vector function of a scalar variable, we can easily adapt the argument of the usual scalar calculus and prove the theorems associated with continuity in that calculus. If $r = f(t)$ be the function considered, t being the scalar variable, we can prove in particular that if $r_1 = f(t_1)$ and $r_2 = f(t_2)$ and ρ is any number such that $|r_1| < \rho < |r_2|$, then there is a value of t lying between t_1 and t_2 for which $|f(t)| = \rho$. In other words, as t varies continuously from t_1 to t_2, the tensor of r assumes at least once every value lying between t_1 and t_2.

It can further be proved that if $F(r)$ is any continuous function, scalar or vector, of r where r itself is a continuous function of a scalar variable t, then F is a continuous function of t.* In case F is a scalar function, it follows that if F_1, F_2 are the values of F respectively for $t = t_1$ and $t = t_2$, then as t varies continuously from t_1 to t_2, F assumes at least once every value lying between F_1 and F_2; and when F is a vector function, it is the tensor of F that assumes, as t varies continuously from t_1 to t_2, at least once every value lying between the tensors of F corresponding to $t = t_1$ and $t = t_2$.

5. If for the continuous vector function $r = f(t)$, a unique limit exists of $\dfrac{f(t') - f(t)}{t' - t}$ as t' approaches t from either side, (*i.e.* from values less than t to t and from values greater than t to t), then this limit is called the differential coefficient of

---

* *Proof.* We have to show that if δ is assigned in advance, η can be found such that

$$1\ F(r') - F(r)\ 1\ \angle\ \delta,$$

when $1\ t' - t\ 1\ \angle\ \eta$, r' being the value of r corresponding to $t = t'$.

Now since $F(r)$ is a continuous function of r, an η_1 can be found such that $1\ F(r') - F(r)\ 1\ \angle\ \delta$, when $1\ r' - r\ 1\ \angle\ \eta_1$.

Again, since r is a continuous function of t, corresponding to this η_1, a positive number η can be found such that $1\ r' - r\ 1\ \angle\ \eta_1$, when $1\ t' - t\ 1\ \angle\ \eta$.

This η then is such that when $1\ t' - t\ 1\ \angle\ \eta$,
$1\ r' - r\ 1\ \angle\ \eta_1$ and $1\ F(r') - F(r)\ 1\ \angle\ \eta$.

r with respect to t and is denoted by $\dfrac{dr}{dt}$. The function r in the same case is said to be differentiable at t.

A function $r = f(t)$ which is continuous and differentiable at all points in a certain region can in general be represented by a curve in that region. The terminus of r will trace out the curve as t goes on varying continuously, and the vector $\dfrac{dr}{dt}$ will be at each point in the direction of the tangent to the curve at that point.

If $F(r)$ is a continuous vector function of r, it follows now from the last article, that the vector diagram of $F(r)$ corresponding to points lying on any arbitrary but continuous curve $r = f(t)$ between any two specified points P and Q is also a continuous curve lying between the corresponding points P′ and Q′ in the vector diagram.

6. *Mean value theorem for* $r = f(t)$.—If r is a continuous and differentiable function of t for all values of t between any two specified numbers t_1 and t_2, then r_1 and r_2 being the values of r respectively for $t = t_1$ and $t = t_2$, we have

$$r_2 - r_1 = \frac{d}{dt} f(t_1 + \theta \,\overline{t_2 - t_1}),$$

where θ is some positive proper fraction.

This is proved, precisely as in the case of the corresponding theorem in scalar calculus, by considering the function

$$\Phi(t) = r - r_1 - \frac{r_2 - r_1}{t_2 - t_1} (t - t_1)$$

which is continuous for all values of t between t_1 and t_2 and vanishes for $t = t_1$ and $t = t_2$, and of which therefore the differential co-efficient will vanish at some point between t_1 and t_2, say at $t_1 + \theta(t_2 - t_1)$, where θ is a positive proper fraction. This proves our theorem.

Graphically, if R denotes the vector to any point on the chord of the curve $r = f(t)$ joining the points t_1 and t_2, the equation of the chord is

$$R = r_1 + \frac{r_2 - r_1}{t_2 - t_1} (t - t_1);$$

for obviously it represents for varying values t a straight line parallel to $r_2 - r_1$ and gives $R = r_1$ at $t = t_1$ and $R = r_2$ at $t = t_2$. Our $\Phi(t) = r - R = R'$, say, represents then for any value of t the difference of the vectors to points on the curve and the chord corresponding to that value of t. If these vector differences are now drawn from the origin for all values of t from t_1 to t_2, their terminii will give us another curve represented by $R' = \Phi(t)$, which clearly is a continuous curve returning unto itself at the origin for $t = t_1$ and $t = t_2$, and the vanishing of $\dfrac{d\Phi}{dt}$ for some intermediate value of t implies that in course of the journey of the terminus of R' from the origin and back to it again, there will be a position which will make the tensor of R' or $r - R$ stationary.

II.

INTEGRALS.

7. *The Vector Volume Integral.*—Given any finite continuous volume τ, if for any convergent system of sub-divisions * of the region, the vector sum $\gtreqless F_\kappa \tau_\kappa$, where τ_κ denotes any sub-region at any stage of the sub-division and F_κ the value of F at any point within the sub-region τ_κ, tends to a definite, unique limit as the sub-division advances, independent of the particular convergent system of sub-divisions used and of the particular values of F chosen within the sub-regions τ_κ, then this limit is called the volume integral of the vector function F through the volume τ, and is written $\int^\tau F d\tau$.

Without going into the question of the necessary minimum condition for the integrability of F, we may prove without much trouble the only theorem we require in this connection, *viz.*, that if F is continuous at all points within a *finite* region, it is integrable also through that region ;— the continuity of F ensuring that if F_κ, $F_\kappa{}'$ are the values of F at any two points in the sub-region τ_κ, the tensor of the difference of F_κ and $F_\kappa{}'$ becomes arbitrarily small as the sub-division advances and each sub-region diminishes in volume.

A graphical representation of the vector volume integral may also be suggested here. Starting from any arbitrary point O', we lay down the vectors $F_\kappa \tau_\kappa$ as in the ordinary polygon of vectors. In the limit the polygon becomes a continuous curve, ending say in $A.'$ Then the arc $O'A'$ will represent $\int |F| d\tau$ and the chord $\overline{O'A'}$ will represent our volume integral $\int F d\tau$. Since F is supposed to be integrable,

---

* Compare Hobson's Theory of Functions of a Real Variable, § 261.

the chord $O'A'$ will be unique, but we may have an infinite number of curves like $O'A'$ according to the different orders in which we may place the vectors $F_n\tau_n$ in forming the polygon. All these curves however will have the same length $\int | F | \, d\tau$ and the same terminal point A'. Further, to any point P' on any one of these curves there will correspond a unique point P in the volume τ, and conversely, so that there is a one-to-one correspondence between the points in the volume and the points on any particular curve.* We have also $d\rho' = Fd\tau$, if ρ' is the vector $O'P'$, so that the tangent at any point P' on the curve is in the direction of F at the corresponding point in the volume. It may happen that $\int | F | \, d\tau$ is infinite, but $\int Fd\tau$ at the same time exists as a finite vector. Thus the curve may make an infinite number of convolutions, but such that the terminal point A' is at a finite distance from O'.

8. *The surface integrals.*—Given any continuous surface S in a region where the vector function F is defined, we form the scalar product $F.n$ at each point of the surface, n denoting the unit vector along the outward normal at any point to the surface, and the surface integral, in the usual sense, of the scalar function $F.n$ over the surface we call the surface integral of vector function F over the surface and denote it by $\int F.ndS$. In other words, for any convergent system of sub-divisions of the surface S, if S_r is a sub-area at any stage of the sub-division and $F_r.n_r$ the value of $F.n$ at any point within the sub-area, the unique limit to which $\geqq F_r.n_r S_r$ is assumed to tend as the sub-division advances is called the surface integral of F over the surface S. But with the advance of the sub-division the areas S_r approximate to small plane areas on the tangent planes at points P, and the vectors $n_r S_r$ ultimately

---

* There is of course no *a priori* absurdity in the idea of a one-to-one correspondence being established between the points in a given volume and the points on a line, for we know from the theory of sets of points that the two aggregates have the same "power."

may be regarded as representing these plane areas both in magnitude and direction. We may replace therefore the notation $\int F.n dS$ ₁by $\int F.d\sigma$, $d\sigma = n dS$ representing the ultimately plane element dS both in direction and magnitude.

Forming again the vector product of F and the vector $n_r S_r$ at each point and summing up for all points and passing to the limit in the same way, we have another surface integral $\int F \times n dS$ or $\int F \times d\sigma$. This has been called the skew or vector surface integral, $\int F.d\sigma$ being the direct or scalar surface integral. We shall always mean $\int F.d\sigma$ when we speak only of the surface integral of F, referring to $\int F \times d\sigma$ as the skew surface integral.

If the surface S is supposed to be continuous and to possess moreover a continuous tangent plane at every point, the vector n would be a continuous function over the surface, and if F is supposed to be continuous also, both F. n and F × n will be continuous functions and the scalar and vector surface integrals of F over S will both exist. We shall always make this supposition here.

9. *The line integrals.*—Given any continuous curve, if in any convergent system of subdivisions, ρ_n is the vector chord joining two consecutive points of division at any stage of subdivision in the system, and F_n is the value of F at any point P of the curve between these two points of division, then the unique limit to which $\geqq F_n.\rho_n$ is assumed to tend as the subdivision advances is called the line integral of F along the curve AB. The chord ρ_n is obviously equal to the difference in the values of r at the two points which it connects, and our integral may be denoted by $\int_A^B F.dr$. It is further clear that with the advance of the subdivision, ρ_n approaches in direction to the tangent to the curve at P, and if therefore we denote the unit vector along the tangent at any point of the curve by t, the integral is the same as the line integral, in the usual

sense, of the scalar function F.t, and might be denoted by ∫ F.t ds, ds being the scalar element of arc.

We might in the same way define the vector line integral ∫ F × dr, but this will rarely occur in the present paper.

In any case we shall always suppose that the curve along which we integrate is not only continuous, but also possesses a continuous tangent, so that t is a continuous vector function of the position of a point on the curve.

The following properties of the line integral follow immediately from the definition.

$$(i) \quad \int_A^B F.dr = - \int_B^A F. dr$$

$$(ii) \quad \int_A^B F.dr = \int_A^P F. dr + \int_P^B F.dr, \text{ P being any point on the}$$

curve AB.

(iii) If l is the length of the arc AB and L, U the lower and upper limits respectively of F.t for the curve AB (which limits are supposed to exist, though not necessarily to be attained), then

$$Ll \leq \int_A^B F. dr \leq Ul.$$

(iv) Further, if M is some number satisfying L≤M≤U, we have $\int_A^B F.dr = Ml$; and in case F is continuous, so that F.t is continuous also, the value M is attained by F.t at some point P of the curve, and we have $\int_A^B F.dr = (F.t) = l.$

III

The Gradient of a Scalar Function.

10. Let F(r) be a continuous scalar function of the position of a point P ($\overline{OP}=r$) in a given region. If Q is a point in the neighbourhood of P, such that $\overline{PQ}=ab$ where a is a unit vector in direction PQ and h a small positive number, then the value of F. at Q is F $(r+ah)$. If now the limit $\underset{h=0}{L}\dfrac{1}{h}$ [F $(r + ah) -$ F(r)] exists as a definite scalar function (different from zero) of a and r, this limit would measure the rate of change in the value of the function for a displacement of P in the direction a. Supposing the limit to exist and denoting it by f (a, r), we have $F(r+ah)-F(r)=hf(a,r)+h\eta$, where η and b have the simultaneous limit zero.

Now since h appears in the left hand side of this equation only in the combination ah, and the first term on the right hand side is linear in h, it follows that this term is linear in a also. The function f (a, r) then is a scalar function linear in a ; it vanishes moreover with a, and therefore it must be of the form a. G (r), where G (r) is a vector function of r, independent of a.

If the limit in question exists now for every direction a emerging from P, the rate of change of F(r) in any direction a is a.G(r), the maximum value of which obviously, for varying directions a, is obtained when a is taken in the direction of G and the magnitude of the maximum value is equal to the tensor of G. The vector G is called the *gradient* of the scalar function F. The gradient of a scalar function then may be generally defined as a vector in the direction of the most rapid rate of increase of the function and equal in magnitude to this most rapid rate.

3

11. The same question may be looked at geometrically also. We begin by proving* that if F (r) is a scalar function continuous in a certain region and does not possess any maxima or minima in the region, and if F_P is the value of the function at any point P of the region, then there passes through P a surface on every point of which F has the value F_P.

For, since P is neither a point of maximum nor minimum, *all* the values of F in the neighbourhood of P cannot be greater than F_P, nor can all the values be less than F_P, and there would be points in the neighbourhood for which F is greater than F_P and there would be points also for which F is less than F_P.

In the neighbourhood of P then, let Q be a point such that $F_Q > F_P$, and R a point such that $F_R < F_P$. Now on account of the continuity of the function, a region can be constructed about Q within which the fluctuation of the function is as small as we please. Hence there exist other points near Q for which also the value of the function is greater than F_P. Similarly there exist points near R for which the function is less than F_P. Hence the region consists of two distinct regions in every point of one of which $F > F_P$, and in every point of the other $F < F_P$.

Again, since in passing from any Q to any R along a continuous curve, F must on account of its continuity assume all the intermediate values, it assumes the value F_P somewhere between

---

* This proof is adapted from the solution an example in Routh's statics, Vol. II (Ex. 2, § 124), where from the fact that gravitational potential is neither a maximum nor a minimum in free space is deduced that an isolated line cannot from part of a level surface.

Q and R on that curve. Hence there is a continuous surface of separation of the two regions at every point of which $F = F_P$, which proves our theorem.

If now the surface possesses a tangent plane at P, we take a point P′ on the normal to the surface at P in its neighbourhood. Through this point P′ also will pass a surface on every point on which $F = F_p′$ and PP′ will be normal to both the surfaces $F = F_P$ and $F = F_{P′}$. Supposing now that the limit $\dfrac{F_{P′} - F_P}{PP′}$

exists as P′ moves continuously along the normal and approaches P, a vector in the direction of this normal and equal in magnitude to the value of this limit is called the gradient of $F(r)$ at P. [P′ might be on the normal on either side of the surface, and it is assumed that the limit in question exists in either case and that these two limits are equal.]

To see that the gradient so defined gives us the most rapid rate of increase of the function both in magnitude and direction, we take a point Q in the neighbourhood of P on the surface on which P′ lies. Let $\angle P′PQ = \theta$. Then the rate of increase of the function in direction PQ

$$= \underset{QP=0}{L} \frac{F_Q - F_p}{PQ} = \underset{PP′=0}{L} \frac{F_p′ - F_p}{PP′} \cdot \frac{PP′}{PQ} = (\text{grad } F) \cos \theta$$

of which the maximum value obviously is obtained when $\theta = 0$. This establishes the identity of the definitions of gradient in the present article and the last.

We denote the gradient by ∇F. If δF is the change in the value of F on account of the shift δr in the position of P, we have

$$\delta F = \nabla F. \, \delta r + \eta \mid \delta r \mid$$

where η and $\mid \delta r \mid$ have the similtaneous limit zero.

12. If the shift δr is supposed to take place along a definite continuous curve $r = \chi(t)$, then as we have seen (§4, p. 10) F would be a continuous function of t along that curve, and our relation of the last article can be written $\dfrac{dF}{dt} = \nabla F. \dfrac{dr}{dt}$.

Further, if t_1, t_2 specify any two points K, L on the curve $r = \chi(t)$ and if F_1, F_2 are the values of F at K and L respectively, we have by the Mean Value Theorem of §6, p.11.

$$F_2 - F_1 = (t_2 - t_1) \left(\frac{dF}{dt}\right)_M$$

where $\left(\dfrac{dF}{dt}\right)_M$ dennotes the value of $\dfrac{d}{dt}F$ at some point M on the curve lying between K and L. .That is to say,

$$F_2 - F_1 = (t_2 - t_1)(\nabla F)_m \cdot \left(\frac{dr}{dt}\right)_M$$

In particular, if the curve is a straight line in the direction of the (unit) vector a and h is the length of KL, so that $\overline{KL} = ah$, we may write $F(r + ah) - F(r) = ha.(\nabla F)_m = ha. \ \nabla F(r + a\theta h)$. where θ is a positive proper fraction; or again, $F(r + a) - F(r) = a.\nabla F(r + \theta a)$.

13. We establish now the corresponding integral formula, for which we prove first that if $f(r)$ is any vector function (not necessarily continuous) integrable along a given curve AB, then

P being any variable point on that curve, the integral $\displaystyle\int_A^P f(r). \, dr$

is a continuous function of the position of P on the curve.

Denote $\displaystyle\int_A^P f(r).dr$ by $F(r)$. Then if Q is any other point

$r + \epsilon$ on the curve, we have $\displaystyle\int_A^Q f(r).dr = F(r + \epsilon)$, and therefore

$$F(r+\epsilon)-F(r)= \int_{P}^{Q} f.dr.$$

But (see p.16) $\left| \int_{P}^{Q} f.dr \right| < Ul$, where U is the upper limit

of $f.t$ for the curve AB and l is the length of the arc PQ.

Hence $| F(r+\epsilon)-F(r) | < Ul$,

and therefore $| F(r+\epsilon)-F(r) |$ can be made less than any arbitrary positive number δ, if only l is so chosen that $\delta > Ul$,

or $l < \dfrac{\delta}{U}$, which is always possible because U is supposed to be

finite. Again, since the curve is supposed to possess a continuous tangent at P (p.16), there is a finite portion of the curve about P for which the arc measured from P and the corresponding chord increase together. It is possible therefore to take a point P' on the curve in such a way that the arc PP' $< \dfrac{\delta}{U}$ and also such that the arcs corresponding to chords PQ which are less than $| \overline{P\ P'} |$, are less than the arc PP' and less therefore than $\dfrac{\delta}{U}$. It follows that for all vectors ϵ satisfying $| \epsilon | < | \overline{PP'} |$, where the arc PP' $< \dfrac{\delta}{U}$, we have $| F(r+\epsilon)-F(r) | < \delta$, which proves our theorem.

14. We conclude that if $f(r)$ is integrable along any curve in a continuous region, and if A is a fixed point and P any variable point in the region, then integrating along the various curves through A and P, we have any number of functions $\int_{A}^{P} f.dr$, each of which is continuous for a displacement of P on

the curve along which the integral is calculated in any case. Under certain conditions however (See §42), of which the continuity of f is one, the intergral is known to be independent of the path of integration, and in this case therefore $\int_A^P f \cdot dr$ will define a unique continuous function $F(r)$ of the position of P in space. Assuming these conditions to hold, and assuming in particular that $f(r)$ is a continuous vector function, we shall prove here that $f = \nabla F$.

For, if f is continuous, and since in accordance with the understanding in § 9, the unit vector t to any curve through A and P is supposed to be continuous, $f \cdot t$ is also a continuous function of the position of a point on this curve. Hence, if P is the point r and we consider another point r' on the curve in the neighbourhood of P, f' and t' being the values respectively of f and t at r', then for any arbitrary δ, a positive number η can be found such that

$$| f' \cdot t' - f \cdot t | < \delta, \text{ if } | r' - r | < \eta,$$

which shows that $| f' \cdot t' |$ lies between $| f \cdot t | + \delta$ and $| f \cdot t | - \delta$; every value, in other words, of $f \cdot t$ in the portion of the curve between r and r' lies between $| f \cdot t | + \delta$ and $| f \cdot t | - \delta$.

If ϵ denotes the vector $r' - r$, the integral $\int_r^{r+\epsilon} f \cdot dr$ lies between

$l[\,| f \cdot t | + \delta]$ and $l[\,| f \cdot t | - \delta]$, l being the length of the arc between r and r'.   •

$$\text{But } F(r + \epsilon) - F(r) = \int_r^{r+\epsilon} f \cdot dr.$$

∴ $F(r + \epsilon) - F(r)$ lies between $l[\,| f \cdot t | + \delta]$ and $l[\,| f \cdot t | - \delta]$ But δ and therefore also l can be taken arbitrarily small; and with the arbitrary shortening of l the difference between the arc l and the chord $| \epsilon |$ becomes arbitrarily small, and the direction of ϵ approximates to that of t. We can write therefore

$F(r+\epsilon) - F(r) = \epsilon \cdot f(r) \pm \mid \epsilon \mid \delta'$, where δ' and $\mid \epsilon \mid$ have the simultaneous limit zero.

This result, which is true for all curves through A and P and true therefore for vectors ϵ drawn in all directions round P shows that $f = \nabla F$.

If therefore we have any curve in the region, and r_1, r_2 are any two points on the curve, we have

$$\int^{r_2} \nabla F \cdot dr = \int^{r_2} f \cdot dr = F(r_2) - F(r_1)$$

IV

The Linear Vector Function.

15. The most general vector expression linear in r can contain terms only of three possible types, r, $a.rb$ and $c \varkappa r$, a, b, c being constant unit vectors. Since r, $a.rb$ and $c \times r$ are in general non coplanar, it follows from the theorem of the parallelopiped of vectors that the most general linear vector expression can be written in the form

$$\lambda r + \mu \, a.rb + \nu c \times r$$

where λ, μ, ν are scalar constants. The constants μ, ν may moreover be incorporated into the constant vectors a and c and we write our general linear vector function in the form

$$\phi \, (r) = \lambda r + a.rb + c \times r,$$

where b only is a unit vector.

Obviously, $\phi \, (r)$ is distributive ;

that is, $\phi \, (a + \beta) = \phi \, (a) + \phi \, (\beta)$,

and further $\phi \, (kr) = k \, \phi \, (r)$, where k is any constant.

16. *Theorem.*—The surface integral of $\phi \, (r)$ over any closed surface S bears a constant ratio to the volume T enclosed by the surface, the constant depending only on the function but being independent of the particular surface over which we integrate.

To prove this we integrate separately the three terms of $\phi (r)$ over the surface.

We know $\int^S \lambda r.d\sigma = \lambda \int^S r.d\sigma = 3\lambda T$.

To calculate $\int^S a.rb. \, d\sigma$ we break up the region S into thin cylinders with axes parallel to b. Since the surface is closed, each of these cylinders like PQ will have an even number of intersections with the surface, as in the usual proof of Green's Theorem. It is enough to consider here the case where there are two intersections only, the extension to the general case being obvious as in that proof. If then $d\sigma'$ and $d\sigma$ are the elements of surface on S enclosed by the cylinder PQ, we have

$b. \, d\sigma' = -b. \, d\sigma =$ area of the cross section of the cylinder PQ.

Let P be the point r, then if x is the length of the cylinder, Q is the point $r+xb$, b being a unit vector; and the sum of the contributions of $d\sigma$ and $d\sigma'$ to the surface integral approximates, as the cross section of the cylinder diminishes, to

$$a.(r+xb) \, b. \, d\sigma'+a. \, r \, b. \, d\sigma$$

$$i.e., \text{ to } a.b \,\, x b.d\sigma'$$

$i.e.$, to $a.bd\tau$, where dT is the volume of the cylinder PQ. Hence the whole surface integral

$$\overset{S}{\int} a.rb.d\sigma = a \cdot b\text{T}.$$

We may just by the way note from the symmetry of the result that $\int a.rb.d\sigma = \int b.ra.d\sigma = a \cdot b\text{T}$, and this result holds for any two arbitrary constant vectors a, b. That is, for any two constant arbitrary vectors a, b we have

$a.\int rb.d\sigma = b.\int a.r \, d\sigma = a \cdot b\text{T}$, which shows moreover that $\int rb.d\sigma = b\text{T}$ and $\int a.rd\sigma = a\text{T}$.

Generally therefore $\int ra.d\sigma = \int a.rd\sigma = a\text{T}$, a being any constant vector.

To return to our proof now, we have to integrate $\int c \times r.d\sigma$. Put $c = a \times \beta$, so that $c \times r = a.r\beta - \beta.ra$ (p. 6)

Hence $\int c \times r.d\sigma = \int a.r\beta \cdot d\sigma - \int \beta.ra.d\sigma = a \cdot \beta\text{T} - a \cdot \beta\text{T} = 0$.

We have therefore finally

$$\int \phi(r).d\sigma = 3\lambda\text{T} + a.b\text{T}$$

$i.e.$, $\frac{1}{\text{T}} \int \phi(r). \, d\sigma = 3\lambda + a.b = \text{D}$, say,

which proves our theorem.

17. The skew surface integral of $\phi(r)$ over any closed surface S divided by the volume T enclosed by the surface is a constant vector, this constant vector depending on the function $\phi(r)$, but being independent of the surface over which we perform the integration.

4

Proof. We proved in the last article that $\int c \times r.d\sigma = 0$, c being any constant vector. It follows that $\int c.r \times d\sigma = 0$ (P. 6),

  i.e., $c.\int r \times d\sigma = 0$, or $\int r \times d\sigma = 0$, because c is arbitrary.

Also, $\int a.rb \times d\sigma = b \times \int a.rd\sigma = b \times aT$ [§16]

Again $\int (c \times r) \times d\sigma = \int rc.d\sigma - \int cr.d\sigma$ [p. 6].

$$= cT - 3cT = -2cT \quad [\S16].$$

Hence $\int \overset{S}{\phi}(r) \times d\sigma = \int \overset{S}{[}\lambda r + a.rb + c \times r] \times d\sigma$

$$= -(a \times b + 2c)T = -CT, \text{ say ;}$$

$$C = -\frac{1}{T} \int \phi(r) \times d\sigma = \frac{1}{T} \int d\sigma \times \phi(r) \text{ being a constant vector,}$$

our theorem is established.

D and C which we find here associated with every linear vector function, we shall always refer to as the **scalar** and **vector constants** respectively of the linear vector function.

18. We consider the function now

$$\lambda r + b.ra - c \times r$$

which is immediately seen to have the same scalar constant $3\lambda + a.b$ as the original function $\phi(r) = \lambda r + a.rb + c \times r$; and its vector constant is $-(a \times b + 2c)$ which differs only in sign from the vector constant of $\phi(r)$.

Further, if a, β are any two arbitrary vectors, we have $a.\phi(\beta) = a.[\lambda\beta + a.\beta b + c \times \beta]$

$$= \beta.[\lambda a + b.aa - c \times a] = \beta.\phi'(a), \text{ if we call the new function}$$
$\phi'(r)$.

The two functions $\phi(r) = \lambda r + a.rb + c \times r$

$$\text{and } \phi'(r) = \lambda r + b.ra - c \times r$$

may on this account be called conjugate functions.

With every linear vector function $\phi(r)$ then is associated another function $\phi'(r)$, characterised by the propery $a.\phi(\beta) = \beta.\phi'(a)$ for any two arbitrary vectors a,β and having further the same scalar constant as $\phi(r)$ and a vector constant differing only in sign from that of $\phi(r)$.

19. Since the scalar or vector constant of the sum (or the difference) of two linear vector functions ' is obviously the sum (or difference) of the scalar or vector constants of the two functions, it follows that the scalar constant of $\phi(r)+\phi'(r)$ is 2D and its vector constant is zero; and that the scalar constant of $\phi(r)-\phi'(r)$ is zero and its vector constant is 2C.

Obviously again the conjugate of $\phi(r)+\phi'(r)$ is itself; this function, that is to say, is self conjugate. And the conjugate of $\phi(r)-\phi'(r)=\phi'(r)-\phi(r)=-[\phi(r)-\phi'(r)]$, which is the original function with the minus sign prefixed. Such a function has been called skew or anti-self-conjugate.

The function $\phi(r)-\phi'(r)$ in full is

$$a.rb-b.ra+2c\times r$$
$$=(a\times b)\times r+2c\times r \quad [\text{p. } 6]$$
$$=(a\times b+2c)\times r=C\times r.$$

Hence $\phi(r)$ can be written

$$=\tfrac{1}{2}[\phi(r)+\phi'(r)]+\tfrac{1}{2}[\phi(r)-\phi'(r)]$$
$$\cdot=\phi_o(r)+\tfrac{1}{2}C\times r, \quad \text{where } 2\phi_o(r) \text{ has been written}$$

for the self conjugate function $\phi(r)+\phi'(r)$.

Any linear vector function $\phi(r)$ therefore can be expressed as the sum of two other functions one of which is self conjugate, has the same scalar constant as $\phi(r)$ and no vector constant, and the other is skew, has no scalar constant and the same vector constant as $\phi(r)$.

The result $\phi(r)-\phi'(r)=C\times r$ shows moreover that the vector constant of all self conjugate functions is zero.

20. The vector constant of $\phi(r)$ may be exhibited in another manner, for which we calculate first the gradient of the scalar function $r.\phi(r)$.

Since $\delta[r.\phi(r)]=(r+\delta r).\phi(r+\delta r)-r.\phi(r)$

$$=(r+\delta r).[\phi(r)+\phi(\delta r)]-r.\phi(r)$$
$$=r.\phi(\delta r)+\delta r.\phi(r)+\delta r.\phi(\delta r)$$
$$=\delta r.[\phi'(r)+\phi(r)]+\eta \mid \delta r \mid, \text{ where } \eta \text{ is}$$

a scalar number which has limit zero as $|\,\delta r\,|$ tends to vanish, it follows that $\nabla[r.\phi(r)]=\phi(r)+\phi'(r)$, and we can write

$$\phi(r)=\tfrac{1}{2}\nabla[r.\phi(r)]+\tfrac{1}{2}C\times r.$$

Integrating now round any plane closed curve, we have

$$\int\phi(r).dr=\tfrac{1}{2}\int\nabla[r.\phi(r)].dr+\tfrac{1}{2}\int C\times r.dr.$$

Since $r.\phi(r)$ is single valued, the first integral on the right hand side is zero, because it is equal to the difference in the values of $\tfrac{1}{2}\,r.\phi(r)$ at the same point before and after circuiting. [p.23.]

Also $\int r\times dr$ is twice the vector area enclosed by the curve, a fact which becomes obvious by taking a new origin O' in the plane of the curve. For if $\overline{OO'}=a,\ \overline{OP}=r$ and $\overline{O'P}=\rho$, we have $r=\rho+a$ and $dr=d\rho,$ and $\int r\times dr=\int(\rho+a)\times d\rho.$ Hence since $\int d\rho$ and therefore also $\int a\times d\rho$ vanishes, the curve being closed, we have $\int r\times dr=\int\rho\times d\rho$ which is a vector normal to the plane of the curve and equal in magnitude to twice its area.

Thus $\int\phi(r).dr=\tfrac{1}{2}\int C\times r.dr=\tfrac{1}{2}C.\int r\times dr=C.n\text{S},$ where S stands for the area enclosed by the curve and n a unit vector along the normal to the plane of the curve.

The ratio $\dfrac{1}{S}\ \int\phi(r).dr=C.n$ does not then depend on the particular curve round which we integrate, but it depends on the orientation of the plane of the curve, on the vector n. This ratio obviously again attains its maximum value when n is taken in the direction of C. The vector constant of $\phi(r)$ then is a vector in the direction of the normal to that plane, round any curve on which if we calculate the line integral of $\phi(r)$ the ratio of this integral to the area of the curve is maximum, and the magnitude of the vector constant is equal to this maximum ratio.

21. There is just one bit of work more in connection with linear vector functions before we are ready for the Differential Calculus of vector functions.

If a is any constant vector, $a\times\phi(r)$ is of course also a linear vector function of r. We proceed to find D_1 and C_1 the scalar and vector constants of $a\times\phi(r)$.

Integrating over any closed surface (enclosing volume T) we have by definition

$$D_1 T = \int a \times \phi(r).d\sigma$$

$$= a.\int \phi(r) \times d\sigma$$

$$= -a.C \ T, \text{ where C is the vector constant of } \phi(r).$$

$$\therefore D_1 = -a.C.$$

Again, $-C_1 T = \int [a \times \phi(r)] \times d\sigma$

$$= \int \phi(r)a.d\sigma - \int a\phi(r).d\sigma \ (\text{p. } 6),$$

But $\int a\phi(r).d\sigma = a\int \phi(r).d\sigma = aDT$, D being the scalar constant of $\phi(r)$.

Also $\int \phi(r)a.d\sigma$ is calculated immediately by breaking up the volume into thin cylinders with axes parallel to a, as in §16, p. 25. Thus if OP$=r$ and PQ$=xa$, the sum of the contributions of the elements of area $d\sigma$ and $d\sigma'$ at P and Q approximates, as the cross section of the cylinder PQ diminishes, to

$$\phi(r+xa) \ a.d\sigma' + \phi(r)a.d\sigma$$

which again, since $xa.d\sigma' = -xa.d\sigma = $vol. of the cylinder

and $\phi(r+xa) = \phi(r) + x\phi(a),$

approximates to $\phi(a)dT$, T being the volume of the cylinder PQ. Hence $\int \phi(r)a.d\sigma = \phi(a)T$

Hence finally $-C_1 T = \phi(a)T - aDT$

$$\therefore \quad C_1 = Da - \phi(a).$$

V

The Differential Calculus of Vector Functions.

22. The Differential Calculus of the scalar function of a single (scalar) variable concerns itself with the rate of change of the function with respect to the variable. In considering in the same way the rate of change of a vector function $f(r)$ of the position of a point in space, the first difficulty we meet with is that this rate of change is different for the different directions in which the point P may be shifted. In fact, the position of P being specified in the usual way by the vector r drawn from a fixed origin, a change in the position of P of magnitude h and in the direction of the unit vector a would be denoted by ah, and the change in the value of the function would be $f(r+ah)-f(r)$. The rate of change then in the value of f at P for displacement of P in direction a is

$$\underset{h=0}{\mathrm{L}} \quad \frac{f(r+ah)-f(r)}{h}.$$

In Gibbs' notation this is denoted by $a.\nabla f$; we shall often denote it,—perhaps a little more expressively—also by $d_a f$.

In order that the limit may exist it is necessary that f should be continuous at P in the direction a. For if f is discontinuous in this direction, then however small h might be, $|f(r+ah)-f(r)|$ would be greater than a certain positive number δ and therefore $\left|\dfrac{f(r+ah)-f(r)}{h}\right|$ can be made greater than any arbitrary positive number, and therefore the limit cannot exist. But the continuity of f alone in direction a cannot ensure the existence of the limit, for which it is necessary that the fluctuation of $\dfrac{1}{h}\left|f(r+ah)-f(r)\right|$ as a function of h should be arbitrarily small within a sufficiently small interval on the line a in the neighbourhood of P. The continuity therefore is a necessary though not the sufficient condition for the existence of the limit in question.

But in any case where the limit does exist as a definite function of a and r, it is clear as in § 10, that that function will be linear in a. We may denote therefore $L \dfrac{1}{h}[f(r+ah) - f(r)]$ by $\phi\,(a, r)$, or more simply by $\phi\,(a)$, where $\phi(a)$ stands for a linear vector function of a. The explicit presence of r in $\phi(a, r)$ would serve to bring out the fact that the rates of change of $f(r)$ are given by different linear vector functions at different points P in the region.

If the limit exists for all directions a issuing from the point P,—for which it is of course necessary that f should be continuous at P—we write for any a :

$$d_a f \text{ or } a.\ \nabla f = \phi\,(a),$$

and $f(r+ah) = f(r) + h\phi(a) + h\eta$, where η is a vector such that $|\,\eta\,|$ has limit zero as h tends to vanish.

Or, since $h\,\phi\,(a) = \phi\,(ah)$ [. §15, p. 24], if δf denotes the vector increment of f corresponding to the increment δr of r,

$$\delta f = \phi(\delta r) + \eta\,|\,\delta r\,|\,.$$

23. If the shift δr be supposed to take place along a definite continuous curve $r = x(t)$, then we know (§ 4), that f would be a continuous function of t along that curve and we would write from our relation of the last article that

$$\frac{df}{dt} = L\ \frac{\phi(\delta r)}{\delta t},$$

which, since $\phi(\delta r)$ is a linear vector function of δr,

$$= L\phi\!\left(\frac{\delta r}{\delta t}\right)\quad [\ \S\ 15,\ \text{p. 24}\ ]$$

$$= \phi\!\left(\frac{dr}{dt}\right).$$

Further, if t_1, t_2 specify any two points K and L on the curve $r = x(t)$, and f_1 and f_2 are the values of f at K and L respectively, then we have from the Mean value theorem of §6,

$$f_2 - f_1 = (t_2 - t_1)\!\left(\frac{df}{dt}\right)_{\!M},$$

where $\left(\dfrac{df}{dt}\right)_M$ denotes the value of $\dfrac{df}{dt}$ at some point M on the curve lying between K and L. In other words

$$f_2 - f_1 = (t_2 - t_1) \left[\phi\left(\dfrac{dr}{dt}\right) \right]_M,$$

if, of course, a definite ϕ exists at every point on the curve between K and L.

In particular, if the curve is a straight line in the direction of the (unit) vector a and h is the length of KL so that $\overline{KL} = ah$, we may write $f(r + ah) - f(r) = h\,\phi(a,\ r + a\theta h)$

$$= h d_a f(r + a\theta h),$$

assuming, of course, that $d_a f$ exists at all points on the line KL.

24. We shall practically always confine ourselves to functions which are not only continuous within a certain region, but are also such that $d_a f$ or $\phi(a)$ exists at every point P of the region for all directions a round that point. If we construct a sphere of unit radius with P as centre, then every point on this sphere will represent a definite direction a issuing from P, and ϕ being known for P would mean that corresponding to every point on the unit sphere we know the rate of change of f (at P) both in direction and magnitude. But as to the rate of change of f at P *as a whole*, we cannot as yet form any definite conception, not at least directly from our knowledge of the function ϕ at P which only brings before our minds a bewildering diversity of the rates of change for the infinitely many directions round P. What we naturally do therefore is to have an idea of some sort of *average* value of ϕ (a) for these directions a,—average of ϕ (a) over the unit sphere round P.

We consider then two kinds of such an average value.

Since a is a unit vector, the magnitude of the component of $\phi(a)$ in direction a is $a.\phi(a)$. We consider first the average of this magnitude over the unit sphere, which is

$$\frac{\int a \cdot \phi(a)\ dS}{S}$$

where dS is the scalar element of area on the surface of the sphere at the terminus of the vector a, and S is the whole surface S.

Since the radius of the sphere is unity, S is equal to 4π and is therefore equal to 3T, where T is the volume of the sphere. Also adS$=d\sigma$ the vector element of area, the normal to the sphere at the terminus of a being along a. Hence the average value

$$= \frac{\int \phi(a) . d\sigma}{3T} = \tfrac{1}{3} D$$

where D is the scalar constant of the linear vector function $\phi(a)$. [D is a constant here in the sense of being independent of a, but is of course a function or r and is different from point to point].

The average rate of change of $f'(r)$ then in the direction of the displacement of P is proportional to the scalar constant of $\phi(a)$, and this average rate therefore for each point of the sphere may be constructed geometrically by making the sphere bulge out uniformly outwards from its centre P by an extra length proportional to D.

To have an idea now of the average value of the tangential component of $\phi(a)$ for all the points of the sphere, we consider naturally the average value over the sphere of the moment of $\phi(a)$ about the centre P. This moment being $a \times \phi(a)$, our average value

$$= \frac{\int a \times \phi(a) dS}{S} = \frac{\int d\sigma \times \phi(a)}{S} = \tfrac{1}{3} C$$

where C is the vector constant of $\phi(a)$, in the present instance of course the constant being a function of r. The average moment therefore is in the direction of C and in magnitude is proportional to that of C. It follows that the average tangential component of $\phi(a)$ on the sphere,—the average of the component that is to say, perpendicular to a,—is perpendicular to C and in magnitude is proportional to that of C. The vector constant of $\phi(a)$ affords us a knowledge of the average rate of change

5

of $f'(r)$ for any small displacement of r, perpendicular to that displacement.

The scalar and vector constants of $\phi(a)$ therefore may be regarded as supplying us with a basis of comparison of the rates of change of $f(r)$ at the various points of the region, and serve in a sense the same purpose that is served by our old $\dfrac{dy}{dx}$ in the case of scalar function of a single (scalar) variable x.

25. The scalar D and the vector C being then so fundamental in the Differential Calculus of Vector Functions, we hasten to exhibit them directly in terms of the function $f(r)$ to which they belong, and we shall find incidentally how they are ultimately identified with the well known Divergence and Curl of the vector function $f(r)$.

26. *Divergence.* We integrate $\int f . d\sigma$ over any small closed surface surrounding the point P. At any point Q on this surface, $\overline{PQ}$ being δr, the value of f

$$=f_P+\phi(\delta r)+h\eta$$

where h stands for $\mid \delta r \mid$ and η is a vector such that $\mid \eta \mid$ has a zero limit as h approaches zero.

Hence $\int f . d\sigma = \int [f_P + \phi (\delta r) + h\eta] . d\sigma$.

But $\int f_P . d\sigma = f_P . \int d\sigma = 0$, the surface being closed ;

$\int \phi(\delta r) . d\sigma = DT$, D being the scalar constant of $\phi (\delta r)$ regarded as a linear vector function of δr and T the volume enclosed by the closed surface.

Also $\int h\eta . d\sigma \not> \int h \mid \eta \mid dS$, dS being the scalar magnitude of $d\sigma$

$< \bar{\eta} \int h ds$, where $\bar{\eta}$ is the greatest value of $\mid \eta \mid$.

But $\int h dS = \kappa T$, where κ is a finite number.

Therefore, $\int h\eta . d\sigma < \bar{\eta} \kappa T$.

Hence $\dfrac{1}{T} \int f . d\sigma - D < \bar{\eta} \kappa$.

.Now let the surface shrink up to the point P in any manner. Then since when h approaches zero, all $\mid \eta \mid$'s and therefore also $\overline{\eta}$ tend to limit zero, it follows that $L \frac{1}{T} \int f.d\sigma$ exists and is equal to D. We have the following definition then—

Enclose the point P by any small closed surface and calculate the integral $\int f.d\sigma$. If the limit of $\frac{1}{T} \int f.d\sigma$ exists as the surface shrinks up to the point P, which limit moreover is independent of the original surface and of the manner of its approach to zero, then this limit is called the divergence of $f(r)$ at P. This limit exists if $\phi(a)$ exists at P, and in this case the divergence of $f(r)$ is equal to the scalar constant of $\phi(a)$, and may therefore be taken (but for the constant factor $\frac{1}{3}$) as the measure of the average rate of change of $f(r)$ corresponding to any displacement of P in the direction of that displacement, the average being taken for all directions round P.

We shall always denote the divergence of $f(r)$ by $\nabla . f(r)$.

27. It is perhaps possible for the divergence of a given function to exist at a given point P without $\phi(a)$ necessarily existing there. Directly, the necessary and sufficient condition for the existence of the divergence at P is that within a sufficiently small neighbourhood of P, the function $\frac{1}{T} \int^{S} f.d\sigma$ should vary continuously for continuous variations of the surface S. In other words, given any arbitrary positive number δ, it should be possible to find a positive number η such that S_1, S_2 being any two closed surfaces round P and T_1, T_2 the volumes enclosed by them,

$$\left| \frac{1}{T_1} \int_1^{S_1} f.d\sigma - \frac{1}{T_2} \int_2^{S_2} f.d\sigma \right|$$

should be less than δ, whenever the surfaces S_1, S_2 are entirely contained within the sphere with centre P and radius η. It is a matter for investigation now how far this condition necessarily implies the existence of $\phi(a)$ at P. We consider however just now only those functions for which $\phi(a)$ exists at every point and for which therefore there is no question as to the existence of the divergence.

28. *Curl.*—Integrating $\iint f \times d\sigma$ over any closed surface in the same way, we have

$$\iint f \times d\sigma = \int [f_P + \phi(\delta r) + h\eta] \times d\sigma.$$

But $\iint f_P \times d\sigma = f_P \times \int d\sigma = 0$, the surface being closed ;

$\int \phi(\delta r) \times d\sigma = -\text{CT}$, C being the vector constant of $\phi(\delta r)$ as a linear vector function of δr.

Also $\int h\eta \times d\sigma \not> \int h \mid \eta \mid d\text{S}$

$$< \overline{\eta} \int h d\text{S}$$

that is, $< \overline{\eta} \kappa \text{T}$

$\therefore \dfrac{1}{\text{T}} \int f \times d\sigma + \text{C} < \overline{\eta} \kappa$, and therefore in the limit when the surface shrinks up to the point P, we have

$$\text{L} \frac{1}{\text{T}} \iint f \times d\sigma = -\text{C}.$$

In general, if we find that the limit of $\dfrac{1}{\text{T}} \int d\sigma \times f$ exists as the surface shrinks up to the point P, the limit so obtained being independent of the original surface and of the sequence of forms taken by it during its approach to zero, then this limit is called the curl of the function $f(r)$ at P. What we have proved above shows therefore that if $\phi(a)$ exists at P, the curl does so too and in this case is equal to the vector constant of $\phi(a)$. For any displacement of P then, the average (for displacements in all directions round P) of the component rate of change of $f(r)$ perpendicular to the direction of the displacement is perpendicular to the curl, and the magnitude of the average is proportional to that of the curl.

29. The curl may also be exhibited in another (the more usual) manner corresponding to the property of the vector constant indicated in § 20, p. 28.

Thus, integrating $\int f.\ dr$ round any small closed plane curve surrounding P, we have

$$\int f \cdot dr = \int [f_P + \phi(\delta r) + h\eta].dr.$$

But $\int f_P \cdot dr = f_P \cdot \int dr = 0$, the curve being closed.

$\int \phi(\delta r) \cdot dr = C \cdot nS$, S being the area enclosed by the curve and n a unit vector normal to the curve. [§ 20].

Also, $\int h\eta \cdot dr \ngtr \int h \mid \eta \mid ds, ds$ being the magnitude of the vector element of arc dr ;

and $\int h \mid \eta \mid ds < \overline{\eta} \int h dS$, $\overline{\eta}$ being as before the greatest $\mid \eta \mid$, and also $\int h ds = \kappa S$, where κ is a finite number.

$$\therefore \int h\eta \cdot dr < \overline{\eta}\, \kappa S,$$

and we have $\dfrac{1}{S} \int f \cdot dr - C \cdot n < \overline{\eta}\, \kappa.$

Hence, as the curve contracts to a point in any manner, $\dfrac{1}{S} \int f \cdot dr$ approaches the unique limit $C \cdot n$. The limit moreover exists for all aspects of the plane area, for all vectors n. These various limits [for the different aspects of the plane have again a maximum value when n is in the direction of C, that is, when the plane is taken perpendicular to C and the magnitude of this maximum value is equal to that of C.

In case therefore $\phi(a)$ exists for the function $f(r)$ at a point P, it is indifferent whether we define the curl as we have already done it, or use the following definition.—

Having described any plane closed curve surrounding the point P, if we find that the limit of $\dfrac{1}{S} \int f \cdot dr$, as the curve contracts to the point P, exists and is independent of the form of the curve and of the manner of its approach to zero, but dependent on the orientation of the plane of the curve, and if further, as this orientation is varied, the various similar limits so obtained for the different orientations all exist and acquire a maximum value for a certain orientation, then a vector drawn perpendicular to the particular plane which gives us the maximum value and equal in magnitude to this maximum value is the curl of $f(r)$ at P.

We shall denote the curl of $f(r)$ by $\nabla \times f(r)^{.}$

30. *Some Transformation Formulae.*—The explicit recognition of the divergence and curl of a given function as the scalar and vector constants respectively of the linear vector function $\phi(a, r)$, which defines the rate of change of the function for displacement in any direction a, considerably facilitates the manipulation of these operators in practical work. This is what we proceed to illustrate.

We shall in this article denote by u a continuous scalar function possessing a gradient at every point within the region considered, and U and V will stand for two continuous vector functions of which the rates of change at any point P will be denoted by the linear vector functions $\psi(a, r)$ and $\phi(a,r)$ respectively, so that the scalar and vector constants of $\psi(a)$ will be $\nabla.U$ and $\nabla \times U$ respectively, and those of $\phi(a)$ will be $\nabla.V$ and $\nabla \times V$ respectively.

(*i*) To show now that
$$\nabla.(uV)=u\nabla.V+\nabla u.V.$$
and $\nabla \times (uV)=u\nabla \times V+\nabla u \times V.$

Proof. Q being a point in the neighbourhood of $P(\overline{PQ}=ah)$, if the values of u and V at Q are $u+\delta u$ and $V+\delta V$, the rate of change of uV for a displacement in direction a

$$= \underset{h=o}{L} \frac{1}{h} [(u+\delta u)(V+\delta V)-uV]$$

$$= \underset{h=o}{L} \frac{1}{h} [u\delta V+V\delta u+\delta u\delta V]$$

$$=u\phi(a)+Va.\nabla u$$

But $\nabla \cdot (uV)$ and $\nabla \times (uV)$ are the scalar and vector constants of this rate regarded as a linear vector function of a. Remembering therefore that the scalar constant of $a.rb$ is $a.b$ [p. 25] and that its vector constant is $a \times b$ [p. 26], we have immediately

$$\nabla \cdot (u\mathrm{V}) = u\nabla \cdot \mathrm{V} + \nabla u \cdot \mathrm{V}$$

and $\nabla \times (u\mathrm{V}) = u\nabla \times \mathrm{V} + \nabla u \times \mathrm{V}$.

(*ii*) To show that

$$\nabla \cdot (\mathrm{U} \times \mathrm{V}) = \mathrm{V} \cdot \nabla \times \mathrm{U} - \mathrm{U} \cdot \nabla \times \mathrm{V}$$

and $\nabla \times (\mathrm{U} \times \mathrm{V}) = \mathrm{U}\nabla \cdot \mathrm{V} - \mathrm{V}.\nabla \cdot \mathrm{U} + \psi(\mathrm{V}) - \phi(\mathrm{U})$

Proof. The rate of change of $\mathrm{U} \times \mathrm{V}$ for the displacement ah of the point P

$$= \mathrm{L}\, \frac{1}{h} [(\mathrm{U} + \delta\mathrm{U}) \times (\mathrm{V} + \delta\mathrm{V}) - \mathrm{U} \times \mathrm{V}]$$

$$= \mathrm{L}\, \frac{1}{h}\, [\mathrm{U} \times \delta\mathrm{V} + \delta\mathrm{U} \times \mathrm{V} + \delta\mathrm{U} \times \delta\mathrm{V}]$$

$$= \mathrm{U} \times \phi(a) + \psi(a) \times \mathrm{V}\,;$$

and we have to find the scalar and vector constants of this as a linear vector function of a.

We recall [§ 21, p. 29] that the scalar and vector constants of $a \times \phi(r)$ are $-a \cdot \mathrm{C}$ and $\mathrm{D}a - \phi(a)$ respectively. Hence

$$\nabla \cdot (\mathrm{U} \times \mathrm{V}) = -\mathrm{U} \cdot \nabla \times \mathrm{V} + \mathrm{V} \cdot \nabla \times \mathrm{U}$$

and $\nabla \times (\mathrm{U} \times \mathrm{V}) = \mathrm{U}\nabla \cdot \mathrm{V} - \phi(\mathrm{U}) - \mathrm{V}\nabla \cdot \mathrm{U} + \psi(\mathrm{V}).$

$$= \mathrm{U}\nabla \cdot \mathrm{V} - \mathrm{U} \cdot \nabla\mathrm{V} - \mathrm{V}\nabla \cdot \mathrm{U} + \mathrm{V} \cdot \nabla\mathrm{U}.$$

(*iii*) We may quite easily prove also the formula for $\nabla(\mathrm{U} \cdot)\mathrm{V}$ as given in Gibbs, Vector Analysis, p. 157, *viz.*

$$\nabla(\mathrm{U} \cdot \mathrm{V}) = \mathrm{U} \times (\nabla \times \mathrm{V}) + \mathrm{V} \times (\nabla \times \mathrm{U}) + \mathrm{U} \cdot \nabla\mathrm{V} + \mathrm{V} \cdot \nabla\mathrm{U}.$$

Thus the rate of change of $\mathrm{U} \cdot \mathrm{V}$ for the displacement ah of the point P

$$= \mathrm{L}\, \frac{1}{h}\, [(\mathrm{U} + \delta\mathrm{U}) \cdot (\mathrm{V} + \delta\mathrm{V}) - \mathrm{U} \cdot \mathrm{V}]$$

$$= \mathrm{L}\, \frac{1}{h}[\mathrm{U} \cdot \delta\mathrm{V} + \delta\mathrm{U} \cdot \mathrm{V} + \delta\mathrm{U} \cdot \delta\mathrm{V}]$$

$$= \mathrm{U} \cdot \phi(a) + \mathrm{V} \cdot \psi(a).$$

Now we know that if this rate of change can be written in the form $a.\mathrm{G}.$, then $\mathrm{G} = \nabla(\mathrm{U} \cdot \mathrm{V}.)$

But $\mathrm{U} \cdot \phi(a) + \mathrm{V} \cdot \psi(a)$

$= \mathrm{U} \cdot [\phi(a) - \phi'(a)] + \mathrm{V} \cdot [\psi(a) - \psi'(a)] + \mathrm{U} \cdot \phi'(a) + \mathrm{V} \cdot \psi'(a)$

$= \mathrm{U} \cdot (\nabla \times \mathrm{V}) \times a + \mathrm{V} \cdot (\nabla \times \mathrm{U}) \times a + a \cdot \phi(\mathrm{U}) + a \cdot \psi(\mathrm{V})$ [p. 27]

$= a \cdot [\mathrm{U} \times (\nabla \times \mathrm{V}) + \mathrm{V} \times (\nabla \times \mathrm{U}) + \phi(\mathrm{U}) + \psi(\mathrm{V})]$

Hence $\nabla(\mathrm{U} \cdot \mathrm{V}) = \mathrm{U} \times (\nabla \times \mathrm{V}) + \mathrm{V} \times (\nabla \times \mathrm{U}) + \phi(\mathrm{U}) + \psi(\mathrm{V})$

$\qquad = \mathrm{U} \times (\nabla \times \mathrm{V}) + \mathrm{V} \times (\nabla \times \mathrm{U}) + \mathrm{U} \cdot \nabla \mathrm{V} + \mathrm{V} \cdot \nabla \mathrm{U}$

We could write the same result in a more compact form.

Since $\mathrm{U} \cdot \phi(a) + \mathrm{V} \cdot \psi(a)$ could be written directly

$= a.\phi'(\mathrm{U}) \times a \cdot \psi'(\mathrm{V})$, we have

$\nabla(\mathrm{U} \cdot \mathrm{V}) = \phi'(\mathrm{U}) + \psi'(\mathrm{V}).$

In particular, $\nabla(a \cdot \mathrm{V}) = \phi'(a)$, a being a constant vector.

A short note on Bilinear Vector functions.

31.　Before passing on to the Second Derivatives of the vector function $f(r)$, it would be necessary to consider very briefly what are called the Bilinear Vector Functions.

A vector function of two variable vectors' linear in both is called a bilinear vector function.

Generally, a vector function of n variable vectors linear in all of them is called an n-linear vector function.

A bilinear vector function is said to be symmetrical if it remains the same when the two vectors are interchanged. If r, r' denote the two variable vectors, the general symmetrical bilinear vector function can contain only terms of the type $r . \psi(r')\lambda$, where λ is a constant vector and ψ is a self-conjugate linear vector function, so that $r \cdot \psi(r') = r' \cdot \psi(r)$. We write therefore for the symmetrical bilinear vector function

$\phi(r, r') = r \cdot \psi_1(r')\lambda_1 + r \cdot \psi_2(r')\lambda_2 + \ldots\ldots\ldots\ldots\ldots\ldots;$

or, $\phi(r, r') = \sum r \cdot \psi(r')\lambda,$

where all the functions ψ are self-coujugate.

32. Since the scalar constant of $a\cdot rb$ is $a\cdot b$ [p. 25], the scalar constant of $\phi(r,r')$, regarded as a linear vector function of r alone, is $\Sigma\lambda\cdot\psi(r')$, or since the functions ψ are all self-conjugate, this scalar constant,

$$=\Sigma r'\cdot\psi(\lambda)=r'\cdot\Sigma\psi(\lambda),$$

of which again, regarded as a function of r', the gradient is $\Sigma\psi(\lambda)$.

It is now obvious a priori from the symmetry of ϕ (r,r')—and it is verified immediately also—that if we had calculated the scalar constant of $\phi(r,r')$ regarded as a function of r' and then had obtained the gradient of this scalar constant with respect to r, we would have got the same result $\Sigma\psi(\lambda)$. Hence, without ambiguity, we may refer to $\Sigma\psi(\lambda)$ as the gradient of the scalar constant of $\phi(r,r')$. We shall denote $\Sigma\psi(\lambda)$ by Γ.

33. Since again the vector constant of $a.rb$ is $a\dot\times b$ [p. 26], the vector constant of $\phi(r,r')$, regarded as a function of r, is $\Sigma\psi(r')\times\lambda$. We want to write down now the scalar and vector constants of this vector constant $\Sigma\psi(r')\times\lambda$ regarded as a function of r'. We recall that the scalar and vector constants of $a\times\phi(r)$ are—$a\cdot C$ and $Da-\phi(a)$ respectively, where D and C are the scalar and vector constants respectively of $\phi(r)$. Hence, since the functions $\psi(r')$ are all self conjugate and therefore their vector constants are zero, it follows that the scalar constant of $\Sigma\psi(r')\times\lambda$ as a function of r' is zero.

And its vector constant

$$=[\psi_1(\lambda_1)+\psi_2(\lambda_2)+\ldots\ldots]-[\lambda_1 D_1+\lambda_2 D_2+\ldots\ldots\ldots],$$

where D_1, D_2...are the scalar constants respectively of $\psi_1(r)$, $\psi_2(r)\ldots\ldots\ldots$

That is, the required vector constant

$$=\Sigma\psi(\lambda)-\Sigma\lambda D=\Gamma-\Sigma\lambda D$$

And here also the results would have been the same if we had calculated the vector constant of $\phi(r,r')$, regarded as a function of r', and then found the scalar and vector constants of this vector constant as a function of r.

6

We may say then without ambiguity that the scalar constant of the vector constant of $\phi(r,r')$ is zero and that the vector constant of the vector constant of $\phi(r,r') = \Gamma - \Sigma\lambda D$. We shall denote this last by C'.

34. For the bilinear vector function we have now to consider *two* conjugate functions. If we regard it as a function of r alone we have one conjugate function, and we have another when we regard it as a function of r' alone. We denote these two conjugates by $\phi'_r(r,r')$ and $\phi'_r{}'(r,r')$ respectively. These conjugate functions are not necessarily symmetrical. Remembering that the conjugate of $a \cdot rb$ is $b \cdot ra$, we have in fact

if $\phi(r,r') = \Sigma r \cdot \psi(r')\lambda = \Sigma r' \cdot \psi(r)\lambda$

$\phi'_r(r,r') = \Sigma\lambda \cdot r\psi(r')$

and $\phi'_r{}'(r,r') = \Sigma\lambda \cdot r'\psi(r)$;

and we propose now to seek for constants like Γ and C' from these conjugate functions.

Since a linear vector function (of one vector) and its conjugate have the same scalar constant and vector constants differing only in sign, it is obvious that the scalar and vector constants of ϕ'_r regarded as a function of r and of $\phi'_r{}'$ regarded as a function of r' could be written down immediately from the results we have already worked out for $\phi(r, r')$, but they would not obviously also furnish us with anything new. Also $\phi'_r{}'$ is only ϕ'_r with r and r' interchanged. We have to calculate therefore only the scalar and vector constants of ϕ'_r regarded as a function of r'.

Since the functions ψ are all self conjugate, the vector constant in question is zero immediately. And the scalar constant $= \Sigma\lambda \cdot rD = r \cdot \Sigma\lambda D$, the gradient of which with respect to r is $\Sigma\lambda D$. We denote $\Sigma\lambda D$ by Γ'. Thus $\Gamma' = \Sigma\lambda D$ is gradient with respect to r of the scalar constant of ϕ'_r regarded as a function of r' and is also the gradient with respect to r' of the scalar constant of $\phi'_r{}'$ regarded as a function of r.

We thus have two independent constants of the symmetrical bilinear vector function, *viz.* Γ and Γ' and a third C' deducible from them.

If the function is $\phi(r,r') = \sum r \cdot \psi(r')\lambda,$

$$\Gamma = \sum \psi(\lambda)$$

$$\Gamma' = \sum \lambda D$$

and $C' = \Gamma - \Gamma'$

---

35. Now we are in a position to consider repeated operations of the derivative operators.

Denoting $L \dfrac{1}{h} [f'(r+ah) - f'(r)]$, the rate of change of $f(r)$

$h=0$

at P for a small displacement of P in direction a by $\phi_1 (a, r)$,
we consider first of all the rate of change of this function $\phi_1(a,r)$
for any displacement of P. If $a'h'$ is this new displacement,
a' being a unit vector and h' a small positive number, then the
rate of change of $\phi_1 (a, r)$

$$= L \frac{1}{h'} [\phi_1(a, r+a'h') - \phi_1(a, r)]$$

$h'=0$

$$= L \frac{1}{h'} \left[L \frac{f(r+a'h'+ah)-f(r+a'h')}{h} - L \frac{f(r+ah)-f(\tilde r)}{h} \right]$$

$h'=0 \quad h=0 \hspace{4cm} h=0$

$$= L \frac{1}{h'} L \frac{1}{h} [f(r+a'h'+ah) - f(r+a'h') - f(r+ah) + f(r)].$$

$h'=0 \quad h=0$

Assuming that a unique limit exists as h, h' approach zero,
we conclude as in §10, p. 17 that this limit is a vector function
linear both in a and a'. We denote this bilinear vector function
by $\phi_2(a', a, r)$ and call it the second differential linear vector
function for $f(r)$, $\phi_1 (a, r)$ being the first.

By definition then

$$d_a f = \phi_1 (a, r),$$
$$d_a' d_a f = \phi_2 (a', a, r).$$

In the same way,

$$d_a d_a' f = L \frac{1}{h} L \frac{1}{h'} [f (r + a'h' + ah) - f (r + a'h') - f (r + ah) + f (r)].$$

$$h = 0 \quad h' = 0$$

and this would be denoted by $\phi_2 (a, a', r)$.

We see that $d_a' d_a f$ and $d_a d_a' f$ differ only in the order in which h and h' are made to approach zero and under certain circumstances, which may be investigated, the limit operations are commutative and then we should have

$$d_a' d_a f = d_a d_a' f.$$

We prove here only that in case $d_a f$, $d_a' d_a f$ and $d_a d_a' f$ all exist and are continuous within a finite region round P, the commutative property of the limit operations in question certainly holds and we have $d_a' d_a f = d_a d_a' f$.

For, applying the Mean Value Theorem of §23, P. 32 to the function

$$f (r + a'h') - f (r).$$

we have $\quad [f(r + a'h' + ah) - f(r + ah)] - [f(r + a'h') - f(r)]$

$= h d_a [f(r + a'h' + a\theta h) - f(r + a\theta h)]$, θ being a positive proper fraction,

$= h d_a h' d_a' [f(r + a'\theta'h' + a\theta h)]$, applying the same Mean Value Theorem to $f(r + a\theta h)$, θ' being some other positive proper fraction.

In the same way we have

$$[f(r + a'h' + ah) - f(r + a'h')] - [f(r + ah) - f(r)]$$
$$= h' d_a' [f(r + ah + a'\theta'_1 h') - f(r + a'\theta'_1 h')]$$
$$= h' d_a' h d_a [f(r + a\theta_1 h + a'\theta'_1 h')],$$

θ'_1, θ_1 being also positive proper fractions.

Provided only then $r+ah$, $r+a'h'$ and $r+ah+a'h'$ lie within the region where our conditions hold, we have it that whatever h, h' might be,

$$f(r+a'h'+ah)-f(r+a'h')-f(r+ah)+f(r)$$
$$=hh'd_a d_a'[\,f(r+a'\theta'h'+a\theta h)]$$
$$=hh'd_a'd_a[\,f(r+a'\theta'_1h'+a\theta_1 h)].$$

Since again $d_a d_a'f(r+a'\theta'h'+a\theta h)$ and $d_a'd_a f(r+a'\theta'_1h'+a\theta_1 h)$ are supposed to be continuous, they approach the same limit at r, and we have $d_a'd_a f = d_a d_a'f$; or $\phi_2(a',a,r)=\phi_2(a,a',r)$. In other words, ϕ_2 is a *symmetrical* bilinear vector function of a, a'.

36. Since by definition ϕ_2 (a',a,r) regarded as a linear vector function of a' gives us the rates of change of ϕ_1 (a,r) for the directions a', the divergence and curl of this latter function are the scalar and vector constants respectively of $\phi_2(a',a,r)$ as a linear function of a'. We proceed to show now how the second derived functions of $f(r)$ can be obtained from ϕ_2, just as we obtained our first derived functions—the divergence and curl of $f(r)$—from ϕ_1. Since the divergence of $f(r)$ is a scalar, we can have its gradient, and the curl being a vector, we can have *its* divergence and curl. We consider these in order.

37. Let D stand for the divergence of $f(r)$; $D=\nabla.f$. If Q is a point in the neighbourhood of P, such that $\overline{PQ}=ah$, we have for the divergence of f at Q,

$$D+\delta D=\nabla.(f+\delta f)=\nabla.f+\nabla.\delta f$$

$$\therefore \quad \delta D \;=\nabla.\delta f=\nabla.[\phi_1(ah,r)+\eta h]$$

$$\therefore a.\nabla D=\underset{h=o}{L}\frac{1}{h}\nabla\cdot[\phi_1(ah,r)+\eta h]$$

$$=\underset{h=o}{L}\nabla.\left[\frac{1}{h}\phi_1(ah,r)+\eta\right] = \nabla\cdot\phi_1^{-}\,(a,r),\quad \phi_1 \text{ being a}$$

linear vector function of a,

But $\nabla.\phi_1(a,r)$ is the scalar constant of $\phi_2(a',a,r)$ regarded as a linear function of a' and is therefore equal to $a\cdot\Gamma$ [§ 32]. Hence $a.\nabla D = a.\Gamma$, and since a is arbitrary, we have

$$\nabla D = \Gamma,$$

where Γ is the gradient of the scalar constant of $\phi_2(a',a,r)$.

38.   In the same way, if C is the curl of f at P and $C+\delta C$ is the curl at Q, $\overline{PQ}$ as before being ah, we have

$$C = \nabla \times f,$$
$$C + \delta C = \nabla \times (f + \delta f)$$
$$\therefore \delta C = \nabla \times \delta f = \nabla \times [\phi_1(ah,r) + h\eta]$$

and $\therefore d_a C = \underset{h=0}{L}\dfrac{1}{h}\nabla \times [\phi_1(ah,r) + h\eta]$

$$= \nabla \times \phi_1(a,r),$$

which we know is the vector constant of $\phi_2(a',a,r)$ regarded as a linear vector function of a'.

Hence $\nabla.C$ and $\nabla \times C$, which are the scalar and vector constants respectively of $d_a C$ as a linear function of a, are respectively the scalar and vector constants of the vector constant of $\phi_2(a',a,r)$. The former we have proved to be zero [§ 33, p. 41],

that is, $\nabla.\nabla \times f$ is always zero;

and the latter was found to be $\Gamma - \Gamma'$, that is

$$\nabla \times (\nabla \times f) = \nabla D - \Gamma',$$

where Γ' is the gradient with respect to a of the scalar constant of $\phi'_{2a}(a',a,r)$ regarded as a funtion of a'. We shall presently find an interpretation of Γ' directly in terms of f.

39.   It was seen [§ 30, (iii), p. 40] that if

$$d_a f = \phi_1(a,r),$$

then $\nabla(a.f) = \phi_1'(a,r)$, where $\phi_1'(a,r)$ is the linear vector function of a conjugate to $\phi_1(a,r)$.

Hence $\nabla.\nabla(a\cdot f) = \nabla.\phi_1'(a.r)$;

that is, $\nabla.\nabla(a.f)$ is the scalar constant of $d_a'\phi_1'(a,r)$ regarded as a function of a'.

Now $d_a'\phi_1'(a,r) = L\underset{h'=o}{\frac{1}{h'}}[\phi_1'(a,r+a'h')-\phi_1'(a,r)]$

Therefore, β being an arbitrary constant vector,

$$\beta \cdot d_a'\phi_1'(a,r) = L\underset{h'=o}{\frac{1}{h'}}[\beta.\phi_1'(a,r+a'h')-\beta.\phi_1'(a,r)]$$

$$=L\underset{h'=o}{\frac{1}{h'}}[a\cdot\phi_1(\beta,r+a'h')-a.\phi_1(\beta,r)]$$

$$=a.L\underset{h'=o}{\frac{1}{h'}}[\phi_1(\beta,r+a'h')-\phi_1(\beta,r)]$$

$$=a.\phi_2(a',\beta,r).$$

Hence $d_a'\phi_1'(a,r)$ is the conjugate of $\phi_2(a'a,r)$ with respect to a. That is,

$$d_a'\phi_1'(a,r) = \phi'_{2a}(a',a,r)$$

Hence $\nabla.\nabla(a.f) = a\cdot\Gamma'$. [§ 34, p. 42]

That is, the divergence of the gradient of the (scalar) magnitude of the component of f in any direction is equal to the component of Γ' in that direction.

40. Generally, starting from any scalar function u, we may have two second derivatives, the devergence and curl of its gradient $G=\nabla u$.

If $G+\delta G$ devote the gradient at Q, $\overline{PQ}=ah$, we have

$$G+\delta G = \nabla(u+\delta u) = \nabla u + \nabla(\delta u)$$

$$\therefore \delta G = \nabla(\delta u) = \nabla[ha\cdot\nabla u + h\eta]$$

$$= \nabla[ha.G + h\eta]$$

$$\therefore d_a G = L\frac{1}{h}\nabla[ha.G+h\eta] = \nabla(a\cdot G).$$

The divergence and curl of G now are respectively the scalar and vector constants of $d_a G$ as a linear vector function of a.

For shortness' sake the divergence of G, that is, $\nabla.(\nabla u)$ is always devoted by $\nabla^2 u$. We prove now that the curl of **G is always zero.**

For denoting $d_a G$ by $\phi(a)$ for a moment, we know that $\nabla(a.G) = \phi'(a)$; and we have just shown that $d_a G = \nabla(a.G)$

$$\therefore \phi(a) = \phi'(a)$$

In other words, $\phi(a)$ is a self conjugate function and therefore its vector constant is zero.

Hence, $\nabla \times (\nabla u) = 0$.

41. We have thus obtained two second derivatives of a scalar function u, viz., $\nabla \times (\nabla u)$ and $\nabla \cdot (\nabla u)$ or $\nabla^2 u$, of which the first vanishes for all functions u.

For the vector function $f(r)$ we got three second derivatives $\nabla(\nabla \cdot f)$, $\nabla \times (\nabla \times f)$ and $\nabla \cdot (\nabla \times f)$, of which the last vanishes for all functions f and the other two correspond to two of the invariants Γ and C' of the symmetrical bilinear vector function $\phi_2(a', a, r)$.

But there was a third invariant Γ' of $\phi_2(a', a, r)$ which we saw was related to f by the relation

$$\nabla \cdot \nabla(a \cdot f) = a \cdot \Gamma' \text{ or } \nabla^2(a \cdot f) = a \cdot \Gamma',$$

showing that $\nabla^2(a \cdot f)$ is maximum when a is taken in the direction of Γ' and the magnitude of this maximum value is equal to the tensor of Γ'. This suggests the following definition of a fourth second derivative of the vector function $f(r)$.—It is a vector of which the direction is that along which if we calculate the component of $f(r)$, the divergence of the gradient of the (scalar) magnitude of this component is maximum, and of which the magnitude is this maximum value. This, as the relation $\nabla^2(a \cdot f) = a \cdot \Gamma'$ verifies immediately, is of course that old derivative which is so familiar to us in its Cartesian form

$$\left(\frac{\partial^2}{\partial x^2} + \frac{\partial^2}{\partial y^2} + \frac{\partial^2}{\partial z^2} \right) (ui + vj + wk)$$

or $i\nabla^2 u + j\nabla^2 v + k\nabla^2 w$,

u, v, w being the Cartesian components of $f(r)$ and i, j, k as usual unit vectors along the axes. But it is certainly significant how, without consciously seeking for it, we arrive at it all the same from an unbiassed and straightforward examination of $\phi_2(a', a, r)$.

We obviously require now a new notation for this second derivative, for it is not deducible by any repetition of the first derivative operators, *viz.*, the gradient, divergence and curl. As all writers on Vector Analysis,—not excluding mathematicians like Silberstein (Vectorial Mechanics, Chap. I) who constantly advocate the exclusion of Cartesian decomposition from Vector Analysis,—have always defined it by its Cartesian expression which immediately suggest for it the notation $\nabla^2 f(r)$, this $\nabla^2 f(r)$ is the notation that is invariably employed. With this notation now we write

$$\nabla^2 f = \Gamma';$$

$$\nabla^2(a \cdot f) = a \cdot \nabla^2 f$$

and further, $\nabla \times (\nabla \times f) = \nabla(\nabla \cdot f) - \nabla^2 f.$

VI.

INTEGRATION THEOREMS.

42. The characteristic properties of the divergence and curl lead almost immediately to the integration theorems

$$(i) \quad \overset{S}{\int} f.d\sigma = \overset{\tau}{\int} \nabla.f \, d\tau \;,$$

$$(ii) \quad \overset{S}{\int} f \times d\sigma = - \overset{\tau}{\int} \nabla \times f d\tau \;,$$

the integrations extending over the surface S and through the volume T of any finite closed region ; and again

$$(iii) \quad \int f.dr = \int \nabla \times f.d\sigma \;,$$

the surface integral here extending over the surface of any finite unclosed region and the line integral round the contour of the unclosed surface. The function $f(r)$ in all cases is supposed to be finite, single-valued and continuous at all points of the region of integration.

To prove the first theorem :—For any sub-division of the region into smaller closed volumes, we know by the usual argument of the integrals cancelling over the interfaces, (the continuity of f ensuring the equality of the values of f at corresponding points on the two sides of an interface) that

$$\overset{S}{\int} f.d\sigma = \overset{r=n}{\underset{r=1}{\Sigma}} \overset{S_r}{\int} f.d\sigma \;,$$

S, denoting the whole surface of any one of the sub-regions.

If now we have a convergent system of sub-divisions such that at any stage the greatest diameters of all the sub-regions are less than any arbitrary number h, then

$$\overset{S_r}{\int} f.d\sigma = D_r \, \tau_r + \eta_r \tau_r \quad [\; \S 26, \;]$$

where D_r is the divergence of f at some point within S_r, τ_r the volume enclosed by S_r and η_r is a number having limit zero as h tends to vanish. Hence

$$\overset{S}{\int} f.d\sigma = \geqq D_r \tau_r + \geqq \eta_r \tau_r$$

Let us pass to the limit now as the sub-division advances and h therefore diminishes indefinitely.

Now $\geqq \eta_r \tau_r$ is always less than $\bar{\eta} \geqq \tau_r$, $\bar{\eta}$ being the greatest η_r

$\therefore \quad \geqq \eta_r \tau_r \quad < \bar{\eta} \; T.$

But T is supposed to be finite and in the limit $\bar{\eta} = 0$.

$\therefore$ in the limit $\geqq \eta_r \tau_r = 0$.

Also, by definition, the limit of $\geqq D_r \tau_r$ is $\overset{\tau}{\int} D d\tau$ or $\overset{\tau}{\int} \nabla.f d\tau$.

Hence $\overset{S}{\int} f.d\sigma = \overset{\tau}{\int} \nabla.f d\tau$.

In precisely the same way we prove that

$$\overset{S}{\int} f \times d\sigma = - \overset{\tau}{\int} \nabla \times f d\tau.$$

To prove the third theorem, we break up, as usual, the unclosed surface by a network of closed curves. Then having a definite convention as to the sense in which the line integrals are to be calculated round these curves, we prove first of all in the usual way that the line integral round the original contour is equal to the sum of the line integrals round the closed curves that have been drawn on the surface. Hence, using the same sort of argument as used above for proving the first theorem, and by a reference to §29, we prove quite easily that

$$\int f.dr = \int \nabla \times f.d\sigma.$$

Corollary 1. For a closed surface $\int \nabla \times f.d\sigma = 0$, and this affords another proof of the theorem $\nabla.\nabla \times f = 0$ [§ 38, p. 46]; for the closed surface may be taken as small as we please, and then integration theorem (i) will prove the result.

Corollary 2. The line integral round every closed curve in the region will vanish, if and only if $\nabla \times f$ is zero at every point of the region. But if the line integral round any closed curve like ADPEA drawn through the two points A and P is zero, that means that the line integrals $\int_A^P f.dr$ are the same, whether we use the path ADP or the path AEP. Similarly if we connect A and P by any other path like AFP, then since the line integral round the closed curve ADPFA is zero also, it follows that the line integral for the path AFP is equal to that for the path ADP. We conclude that the condition (promised in §14, p. 22) that $\int_A^P f.dr$ may be independent of the path of integration and may therefore define a unique function of P, (A being a fixed point) is that the curl of f should be zero at every point of the region considered.

43. If we put $f = au$ in the theorem (i) of the last article, a being any constant vector and u a continuous scalar function possessing a gradient at every point of the region considered, we have

$$\int ua.d\sigma = \int \nabla .(au)d\tau$$
$$= \int a.\nabla u \, d\tau \; ; [\S \; 30, \, (i) \; \text{p. } 38]$$

that is, for any arbitrary constant vector a, we have

$$a.\int ud\sigma = a.\int \nabla ud\tau.$$

It follows that $\int ud\sigma = \int \nabla ud\tau.$

Again putting $f = au$ in the theorem (iii) of the last article, we have

$$\int u \, a. \, dr = \int \nabla \times (ua). \, d\sigma$$
$$= \int \nabla u \times a. \, d\sigma \quad [\S \; 30, \, (i) \;]$$
$$= \int a. \, d\sigma \times \nabla u,$$

the integrals extending round the contour and over the surface respectively of any unclosed surface.

Since a is a constant vector, we may write

$$a. \int udr = a. \int d\sigma \times \nabla u$$

$$\therefore \quad \int udr = \int d\sigma \times \nabla u, \, a \text{ being arbitrary.}$$

44. *Differential of an integral.*—Since the calculation of the gradient, divergence and curl all depend on that of the differential of the function considered, it is necessary to have formulæ for the differentials of functions given in the form of integrals, before we can get the result of operation on them by these derivative operators.

Let $f(r, \lambda)$ be a vector or scalar function, λ being an arbitrary (vector) parameter of the function.

Consider the volume integral $\int f(r, \lambda)\, d\tau$ of the function, the region of integration being bounded by the surface $F(r, \lambda) = 0$, where F is a scalar function. The integral of course is a function of λ alone, say $\chi(\lambda)$.

Imagine now a small increment $\delta\lambda$ to be given to λ and let τ and τ' denote the volumes bounded by $F(r, \lambda) = 0$ and $F(r, \lambda + \delta\lambda) = 0$ respectively. Then

$$\delta\chi(\lambda) = \int^{\tau'} f(r, \lambda + \delta\lambda) d\tau - \int^{\tau} f(r, \lambda) d\tau$$

$$= \int^{\tau} f(r, \lambda + \delta\lambda) d\tau + \int_{\tau}^{\tau'} f(r, \lambda + \delta\lambda)\ d\tau - \int^{\tau} f(r, \lambda)\ d\tau$$

$$= \int^{\tau} [f(r, \lambda + \delta\lambda) - f(r, \lambda)]\, d\tau + \int_{\tau}^{\tau'} f(r, \lambda + \delta\lambda) d\tau,$$

$\int_{\tau}^{\tau'} f(r, \lambda + \delta\lambda) d\tau$ denoting that this integral is to be taken in the region between the surfaces $F(r, \lambda) = 0$ and $F(r, \lambda + \delta\lambda) = 0$, $d\tau$ being reckoned positive or negative according as it is outside or inside the surface $F(r, \lambda) = 0$.

Now as $|\delta\lambda|$ becomes smaller, the surface $F(r, \lambda + \delta\lambda) = 0$ approaches $F(r, \lambda) = 0$ and the volume between them tends to become a thin shell distributed over this last surface; and if r and $r + \delta r$ are corresponding points on the surfaces $F(r, \lambda) = 0$ and $F(r, \lambda + \delta\lambda) = 0$, the volume $d\tau$ of this shell resting

on the element of area $d\sigma$ at r' on the surface $F(r,\lambda) = 0$
tends to

$$\delta r.d\sigma \text{ or } \delta r.n dS$$

that is, to $\dfrac{\delta r.\nabla_r F(r,\lambda)}{|\nabla_r F|} dS,$

n the unit vector along the normal to $F(r,\lambda) = 0$ being $\dfrac{\nabla_r F}{|\nabla_r F|}$,

if $\nabla_r F$ denotes the gradient of $F(r,\lambda)$ regarded as a function
of r alone.

Hence, as $|\delta\lambda|$ diminishes,

$$\int_\tau^{\tau'} f(r,\lambda+\delta\lambda)\, d\tau$$

tends to $\displaystyle\int\int_{}^{S} f(r,\lambda+\delta\lambda)\ \dfrac{\delta r.\nabla_r F}{|\nabla_r F|} dS$, the surface integral being

taken over the surface S of $F(r,\lambda) = 0$

To express this integral now explicitly in terms of $\delta\lambda$, we note
generally that

$$F(r+\delta r,\lambda+\delta\lambda) - F(r,\lambda)$$

$$= F(r+\delta r,\lambda+\delta\lambda) - F(r,\lambda+\delta\lambda) + F(r,\lambda+\delta\lambda) - F(r,\lambda)$$

$$= \delta r.\nabla_r F(r+\theta\delta r,\lambda+\delta\lambda) + \delta\lambda.\nabla_\lambda F(r,\lambda+\theta'\delta\lambda) \quad [\S\ 12,\ \text{p. 20.}]$$

which, by sufficiently diminishing $|\delta\lambda|$ and $|\delta r|$ may be
made to approximate, to any arbitrary degree of accuracy, to

$$\delta r.\ \nabla_r F(r,\lambda) + \delta\lambda.\nabla_\lambda F(r,\lambda),$$

if of course both $\nabla_r F$ and $\nabla_\lambda F$ are supposed to be continuous
functions of r and λ.

If now $r+\delta r$ be supposed to be a point on the surface
$\lambda+\delta\lambda$, in the neighbourhood of the point r on the surface λ,
then

$$F(r+\delta r,\lambda+\delta\lambda) = 0 \text{ and } F(r,\lambda) = 0,$$

and therefore $\delta r.\nabla_r F(r,\lambda) + \delta\lambda.\nabla_\lambda F(r,\lambda)$ can be made arbitrarily
small.

Hence the integral $\int_{\tau}^{\tau'} f(r, \lambda+\delta\lambda)d\tau$ further approximates to

$$-\int f(r, \lambda+\delta\lambda)\frac{\nabla_\lambda F.\,\delta\lambda}{|\,\nabla_r F\,|}d\,S$$

the degree of approximation remaining the same.

We write finally therefore

$$\delta\chi(\lambda) = \delta\int^\tau f(r, \lambda)\,d\tau$$

$$= \int^\tau [f(r, \lambda+\delta\lambda)-f(r, \lambda)]\,d\tau$$

$$- \int^S f(r, \lambda+\delta\lambda)\frac{\nabla_\lambda F.\,\delta\lambda}{|\,\nabla_r F\,|}\,dS.$$

our assumptions about the function F being that both $\nabla_r F$ and $\nabla_\lambda F$ are continuous functions in each of the vectors r and λ.

45. Suppose now f to be a continuous *scalar* function possessing a gradient at every point within the region of integration. Then by the Mean Value Theorem of § 12, p. 20,

$$\delta\int^T f(r,\lambda)d\tau = \int^T [\delta\lambda \cdot \nabla_\lambda f(r,\lambda+\theta_1\delta\lambda)]d\tau$$

$$-\int^S [f(r,\lambda)+\delta\lambda \cdot \Delta_\lambda f(r,\lambda+\theta_1\delta\lambda)]\frac{\nabla_\lambda F.\,\delta\lambda}{|\,\nabla_r F\,|}\,dS \quad.$$

θ_1 being a positive proper fraction.

If we further assume the continuity of $\nabla_\lambda f$ in λ, then since the surface S and the volume T are both supposed to be finite, the difference between the right hand side of the last equation and

$$\int^T [\delta\lambda \cdot \nabla_\lambda f(r, \lambda)]d\tau - \int^S f(r, \lambda)\frac{\nabla_\lambda F.\,\delta\lambda}{|\,\nabla_r F\,|}dS,$$

that is, the difference between this right hand side and

$$\delta\lambda \cdot [\int^T \nabla_\lambda f d\tau - \int^S f\,\frac{\nabla_\lambda F}{|\,\nabla_r F\,|}\,dS]$$

will have limit zero as $|\,\delta\lambda\,|$ tends to vanish. Hence

$$\nabla_\lambda \int^T f((r,\;\lambda)d\tau = \int^T \nabla_\lambda f d\tau - \int^S f\,\frac{\nabla_\lambda F}{|\,\nabla_r F\,|}\,dS.$$

46. Suppose next that f is a continuous *vector* function. Let $d_\alpha f$ denote the rate of change of f, regarded as a function of λ, for an increment of λ in the direction of the unit vector α.

If we assume now that $d_\alpha f$ is a continuous function of λ, then using the Mean Value Theorem of § 23, p. 32, and remembering that the surface S and volume T are finite, we have, by an argument similar to that of the last article.

$$d_\alpha \chi(\lambda) = \int d_\alpha f d\tau - \int f \frac{\alpha \cdot \nabla_\lambda F}{|\nabla_r F|} dS.$$

But the divergence and curl of $\chi(\lambda)$ are the scalar and vector constants respectively of $d_\alpha \chi(\lambda)$ regarded as a linear vector function of α.

Now since the scalar constant of the sum of any number of linear functions is the sum of the scalar constants of those functions, and since further the scalar constant of $d_\alpha f$ is $\nabla \cdot f$, we have the scalar constant of $\int d_\alpha f d\tau = \int \nabla_\lambda \cdot f d\tau$. Hence, [remembering that the scalar constant of $\alpha \cdot rb = a \cdot b$ (p. 25)].

$$\nabla \cdot \chi(\lambda) = \nabla_\lambda \cdot \int^\tau f(r, \lambda) d\tau = \int^\tau \nabla_\lambda \cdot f d\tau - \int \frac{f \cdot \nabla_\lambda F}{|\nabla_r F|} dS.$$

Similarly,

$$\triangle_\lambda X \int^T f(r, \lambda) d\tau = \int^T \nabla_\lambda X \, f d\tau - \int^S \frac{\nabla_\lambda F X f}{|\nabla_r F|} ds.$$

47. If λ is not involved in the equation of the bounding surface, and its variation therefore does not affect the region of integration, we have simply, for a scalar function $f(r,\lambda)$

$$\nabla_\lambda \int^\tau f d\tau = \int^\tau \nabla_\lambda f d\tau \, ;$$

and for a vector function $f(r,\lambda)$

$$\nabla_\lambda \cdot \int f d\tau = \int \nabla_\lambda \cdot f d\tau$$

and $\nabla_\lambda X \int f d\tau = \int \nabla_\lambda X f d\tau$,

the restrictions imposed on f being the same, *viz.*, that both f and δf should be continuous functions.

48. We conclude our vector calculus here. A much greater elaboration of details would certainly have been necessary, if it had been intended to present the subject with any degree of completeness for purposes of practical applications. There are certain obvious extensions moreover which suggest themselves immediately from the work done here in the foregoing pages; for example,

(*i*) The discussion of the trilinear, and generally of the *n*-linear symmetrical vector fuctions with a view to discovering the higher derivative operators.

(*ii*) The discussion of the improper integrals,—in particular integrals of functions having one or more infinities in the region of integration, and of finite functions through regions extending to infinity, and the differentials of such integrals; and of Poisson's equation for vector functions.

(*iii*) The consideration of what Gibbs calls the determinant of the linear vector function, and the development therefrom of the Jacobian and Hessian of vector functions on the same lines that have been adopted here for developing the ideas of divergence and curl from what we have called the scalar and vector constants of the linear vector function.

But the object throughout the present paper has been to bring into as great a prominence as possible the one idea that the concepts of divergence and curl of a vector function,—which we are always in the habit of thinking of in terms of those physical ideas that gave rise to them,—do also form, quite apart from their physical interpretations, the fundamental notions of the Abstract Calculus of Vectors, and supply us with a counterpart of the differential co-efficient of a scalar function in the very real sense of giving us a basis of comparison of the rates of change of the vector function from point to point of the field; and further that this new mode of viewing them introduces considerable simplicity in the practical work of manipulation of these operators.

PART II

THE STEADY MOTION OF A SOLID UNDER NO FORCES IN LIQUID EXTENDING TO INFINITY.

An attempt is made in this Part II to apply vector methods to the above problem. It is just likely that it will be [found to contain, especially towards the end, some new results which have not yet been worked out either with the cartesian or with vector calculus.

1. The origin O being fixed in the solid, if we denote by the vectors R and G the force and couple constituents of the "impulse" that would, at any instant, produce from rest the motion of the system consisting of the solid and the liquid, and by the vectors V and W the linear and angular velocity components of the solid, then arguing as in Lamb's Hydrodynamics, Chap. VI, §§ 119, 120, we have for the equations of the motion of system,

$$\frac{d\mathbf{R}}{dt} - \mathbf{R} \times \mathbf{W} = \xi,$$
$$\text{and } \frac{d\mathbf{G}}{dt} - \mathbf{R} \times \mathbf{V} - \mathbf{G} \times \mathbf{W} = \lambda, \qquad \qquad . \quad (1)$$

where ξ, λ represent the force and couple constituents of the extraneous forces, the left hand sides being the rates of change of R, G when the 'origin system' [see Silberstein's Vectorial Mechanics, foot note, p. 69] has the velocities V and W.

If T is the kinetic energy of the system, we have

$$2T = V.R + W.G$$
$$\text{and further, } R = \nabla_v T \text{ and } G = \nabla_w T, \qquad \qquad \ldots \quad (2)$$

where $\nabla_v T$ and $\nabla_w T$ denote the gradients of T regarded as a function of V alone and W alone respectively. [Lamb § 122.]

2. We have to express first T in terms of V and W and then equations (2) will give us expressions for R and G in terms of V and W.

If we put T_1 for the kinetic energy of the liquid motion alone and T_2 for the kinetic energy of the solid, $T = T_1 + T_2$ and we calculate T_1 and T_2 separately.

3. To calculate T_1—If U is the velocity potential of the liquid motion, we have, if we take the density of the liquid to be unity.

$$2T_1 = \int U \nabla U.da$$

where the integration extends over the surface of the moving solid.

Now the velocity potential U satisfies the following conditions :—

(i) $\nabla^2 U = O$ at all points of the liquid ;

(ii) $n.\nabla U = n. (V + W \times r)$ at any point P on the surface of the solid, r denoting the vector $\overline{OP}$, and n being a unit vector along the outward normal to the surface at P. —For the velocity of the liquid at the same point is ∇U, and the normal components of these two velocities must be the same.

(iii) $\nabla U = O$ at infinity.

Of these, condition (ii) shows that U must be linear in both V and W. It is also a scalar. Therefore it must be of the form F. V + F.'W, where F.F' are two vector functions of the position of a point (i.e. functions of r), but independent of V and W.

Taking then U = F.V + F'.W, condition (i) becomes

$$\nabla^2 (F.V) + \nabla^2 (F'.W) = O.$$

at all points of the liquid. Or, since V and W are constant vectors so far as the operation of ∇^2 is concerned,

$$V.\nabla^2 F + W \nabla^2 F' = O. \qquad \text{[See page 49.]}$$

Or, again, since V and W are perfectly arbitrary, we have

$$\nabla^2 F = 0 \text{ and } \nabla^2 F' = 0 \qquad . \quad (A)$$

at all points of the liquid.

Again $F.V + F'.W$ being written for U, our condition (ii) becomes $n. \nabla(F.V + F'.W) = n. (V + W \times r)$;

or since V and W are arbitrary.

$$n.\nabla(F.V) = n.V,$$

$$\text{and } n.\nabla(F'.W) = n.W \times r$$

at all points r on the surface of the solid. If for a moment we write $\phi(\delta r)$ and $\psi(\delta r)$ for δF and $\delta F'$ respectively, we have by § 30, p. 40, $\nabla(F.V) = \phi'(V)$ and $\nabla F'.W) = \psi'(W)$, and therefore the above relations may be written

$$n.V = n.\phi'(V) = V.\phi(n),$$

$$\text{and } n.W \times r = n.\psi'(W) = W.\psi(n) ;$$

$$\left. \begin{array}{l} \text{or,} \quad n = \phi(n) = n.\nabla F \\ \\ \text{and } r \times n = \psi(n) = n.\nabla F', \end{array} \right\} \qquad . \quad (B)$$

since V, W are arbitrary.

Thirdly, condition (iii) becomes

$$\nabla(F.V) = 0 \text{ and } \nabla(F'.W) = 0$$

$$\text{or} \quad \psi'(V) = 0 \text{ and } \psi'(W) = 0 \qquad . \quad (C)$$

at infinity for all arbitrary vectors V and W.

Conditions (A), (B) and (C) will uniquely determine the vectors F, F' and so U being determined, we have

$$2T_1 = \int U \nabla U. \ da.$$

$$= \int U(V + W \times r).da, \text{ by the surface condition (ii)},$$

U being written for $F.V + F'.W$.

4. To calculate T_2, the kinetic energy of the solid:—

We have, $2T_2 = \int(V + W \times r) . (V + W \times r) \, dm$, dm being an element of mass of the solid at the point r and the integration extending through the mass of the moving solid.

That is, $2T_2 = \int [V.V + 2V.W \times r + W . (r \times \overline{W \times r})] \, dm$ [see p. 6].

$$= m \, V.V + 2m \, \overline{r}. \, V \times W + W.\omega(W),$$

where m denotes the mass of the solid, $\overline{r}$ the vector to its centre of gravity (so that $\int r \, dm = m \, \overline{r}$), and $\omega (W)$ has been written for $\int r \times (W \times r) dm$. Writing this integral in the form $\int (r.rW - Wr.r) dm$ [p. 6], we see that $\omega (W)$ is a self conjugate linear vector function of W. Clearly also $\omega(W)$ represents what the angular momentum of the solid about O would have been, if O had been fixed; and $W.\omega(W) = $ constant, is, for variable W, the equation of the momental ellipsoid of the solid at O.

5. We can now write down the expression for the kinetic energy of the system in terms of V and W. Thus,

$$2T = 2T_1 + 2T_2$$

$$= \int UV.da + \int UW \times r.da + mV.V + 2m\overline{r}.V \times W + W.\omega(W).$$

For R and G, then, we calculate $\nabla_r T$ and $\nabla_w T$ from this expression for T. Noting that $\nabla(a.r) = a$ and $\nabla(r.\phi r) = 2\phi r$, if ϕ is self conjugate [p. 28], and that $\nabla_r U = F$ and $\nabla_w U = F'$, we write down almost immediately

$$2 \, R = 2\nabla_r T = \int U da + \ \ FV.da + \int FW \times r.da + 2mV + 2mW \times \overline{r}$$

and

$$2 \, G = 2\nabla_w T = \int F'V.da + \int Ur \times da + \int F'W \times r.da + 2m\overline{r} \times V + 2\omega(W).$$

6. There are now certain relations among the integrals occurring in these expressions for R and G. Just to obtain these we prove generally that if V is any constant vector,

$$\overset{S}{\int} FV. \, (da.\nabla F') = \overset{S}{\int} F'.V(da \nabla F),$$

F, F' being any two vector functions, satisfying $\nabla^2 F = 0$ and $\nabla^2 F' = 0$ at all points within the closed surface S over which the integrations are performed.

If we put, as before, $\delta\ F = \phi(\delta r)$ and $\delta F' = \psi(\delta r)$, then $da.\nabla F'$ $= \psi(da)$ and $da.\nabla F = \phi(da)$. If then C is any arbitrary constant vector

$$C.\int^S FV.\ (da.\nabla F') = \int^S F.CV.\psi(da)$$

$$= \int^S F.C\psi'(V).da$$

$$= \int^S F.C\nabla(F'V).da.$$

which by Green's Theorem $= \int^T \nabla.[F.C\nabla\ (F'.V)]\ d\tau$, the volume integral being taken through the volume T enclosed by S. Using now (i) § 30, p. 38, and the relation $\nabla^2 F' = 0$, we have

$$C.\int^S FV.\ (da.\nabla F') = \int^T \nabla(F.C).\ \nabla(F'.V)\ d\tau ;$$

Similarly, $C.\int^S F'.V\ (da.\nabla F) = \int^T \nabla(F.C).\nabla(F'.V)d\tau.$

C being arbitrary, this proves our theorem.

In the application of this theorem to our problem, we have to note that the region of integration would be that between the surface of the solid and a sphere of infinite radius, and the question of convergence of the integrals would arise. This question has been discussed by Leathem in "Volume and Surface Integrals used in Physics," Sections IX and XI.

7. Using this theorem now and remembering our surface condition (B), viz., $\phi(da) = da$ and $\psi(da) = r \times da$, we have, among the integrals in the expressions for R and G in § 5

$$\int FV.\ da = \int FV.\ \phi(da) = \int F.V\phi(da) = \int F.V\ da, \qquad \ldots \quad (a)$$

$$\int FW \times r.\ da = \int FW.\ r \times da = \int FW.\ \psi(da) = \int F'.W\ \phi\ (da)$$
$$= \int F'.W da, \qquad \ldots \quad (\beta)$$

$\int F'V.\ da = \int F'V.\phi(da) = \int F.V\psi(da) = \int F.V_1 \times da,$ ... (γ)

$\int F'W \times r.da = \int F'W.r \times da = \int F'W.\ \dot\psi\ (da) = F'.W\ \psi(da)$
$= \int F'.W\ r \times da$ ... (δ)

Hence those same expressions for R and G may be written

$R = \int U da + mV + mW \times \bar r = [\int F.V da + mV] + [\int F'.W da + mW \times \bar r],$

$G = \int Ur \times da + m\bar r \times V + \omega(W) = [\int F.Vr \times da + m\bar r \times V]$
$+ [\int F'.Wr \times d_1 + \omega(W)].$

We write now $R = \phi_1 V + \phi_2 W$, where $\phi_1,\ \phi_2$ are the two linear vector functions,

$$\phi_1 V = \int F.V da + mV$$
and $\phi_2 W = \int F'.W da + mW \times r.$

Since the conjugate of $a.\ r\ b$ is $a\ r.\ b$, (a) shews that ϕ_1 is self conjugate. The conjugate of $\phi_2 W$

$$= \int F'\ W.\ da - mW \times \bar r$$
$$= \int F.Wr \times da + m\bar r \times W,\ \text{by } (\gamma),$$

so that $\phi'_2 V = \int F.Vr \times da + m\bar r \times V.$ Hence we may write

$$G = \phi'_2 V + \phi_3 W,$$

where $\phi_3 W = \int F'.Wr \times da + \omega(W).$ Since $\omega(W)$ is self conjugate

(p. 78), (δ) shows that ϕ_3 is self conjugate.

Thus we may write

$$\left.\begin{array}{c} R = \phi_1 V + \phi_2\ W \\ \text{and } G = \phi'_2 V + \phi_3 W. \end{array}\right\} \qquad . \quad (3)$$

where $\phi_1,\ \phi_3$ are self conjugate functions.

This fact alone,—of $\phi_1,\ \phi_3$ being self conjugate and ϕ_2 and ϕ'_2 being conjugate—could of course be deduced directly from (2), p. 74.

8. Considering now the case where no extraneous forces are present, we have, putting $\zeta,\ \lambda = 0$ in equations (1) of page 74.

$$\frac{d\mathbf{R}}{dt} = \mathbf{R} \times \mathbf{W},$$

and $\dfrac{d\mathbf{G}}{dt} = \mathbf{R} \times \mathbf{V} + \mathbf{G} \times \mathbf{W}.$

The three well known integrals follow immediately.

(i) Multiplying the first equation scalarly by R, we have

$$\mathbf{R} . \frac{d\mathbf{R}}{dt} = (\mathbf{R}\mathbf{R}\mathbf{W}) = 0$$

$\therefore$ R:R = constant.

(ii) $\mathbf{G} . \dfrac{d\mathbf{R}}{dt} + \mathbf{R} . \dfrac{d\mathbf{G}}{dt} = (\mathbf{G}\mathbf{R}\mathbf{W}) + (\mathbf{R}\mathbf{R}\mathbf{V}) + (\mathbf{R}\mathbf{G}\mathbf{W}) = 0$

$\therefore$ R. G = constant.

That is, the pitch of the wrench (R,G) which is $\dfrac{\mathbf{R}.\mathbf{G}}{\mathbf{R}.\mathbf{R}}$ is constant.

Again, if $r = \dfrac{\mathbf{R} \times \mathbf{G}}{\mathbf{R}.\mathbf{R}}$, which we know is the perp. from O on the axis of the wrench (R,G),

$$\frac{dr}{dt} = \frac{1}{\mathbf{R}.\mathbf{R}} \ [\frac{d\mathbf{R}}{dt} \times \mathbf{G} + \mathbf{R} \times \frac{d\mathbf{G}}{dt}]$$

$$= \frac{1}{\mathbf{R}.\mathbf{R}} [(\mathbf{R} \times \mathbf{W}) \times \mathbf{G} + \mathbf{R} \times (\mathbf{R} \times \mathbf{V}) + \mathbf{R} \times (\mathbf{G} \times \mathbf{W})],$$

which by the last formula of p. 6, reduces to

$$\frac{1}{\mathbf{R}.\mathbf{R}} [(\mathbf{R} \times \mathbf{G}) \times \mathbf{W} + \mathbf{R} \times (\mathbf{R} \times \mathbf{V})],$$

that is, $\dfrac{dr}{dt} = r \times \mathbf{W} - \mathbf{V}_1$

where $\mathbf{V}_1 = -\dfrac{\mathbf{R} \times (\mathbf{R} \times \mathbf{V})}{\mathbf{R}.\mathbf{R}} =$ component of V perpendicular to R.

If then $\left(\dfrac{dr}{dt}\right)$ denote the rate of change of r in space, $\left(\dfrac{dr}{dt}\right)$

$$\equiv \frac{dr}{dt} - r \times W + V = V - V_1 = V_2, \text{ where } V_2 \text{ denotes the com-}$$

ponent of V parallel to R, *i.e.*, to the axis of the wrench (R,G). It follows that this axis is a fixed line in space, its direction being obviously constant from the first of the equations of motion.

But there was no special point deducing these results from the equations of motion, as the fact they express, *viz.*, the constancy of wrench (R,G) in case no extraneous forces act, was obvious *á priori* from the theorem that "the 'impulse' of the motion (in Lord Kelvin's sense) at time t differs from the impulse at time t_0 by the time-integral of the extraneous forces acting on the solid during the interval $t-t_0$."—[Lamb § 119]— of which theorem it is only an analytical expression that we have in the equations of motion.

(iii) $\quad \because 2T = R.V + G.W,$

$$2 \frac{d\tau}{dt} = R.\frac{dV}{dt} + \frac{dR}{dt} V + G.\frac{dW}{dt} + \frac{dG}{dt}.W.$$

Using (3) p. 81, $R.\dfrac{dV}{dt} + G.\dfrac{dW}{dt}$ reduces to $V.\dfrac{dR}{dt} + W.\dfrac{dG}{dt}$

$$\therefore \frac{dT}{dt} = V.\frac{dR}{dt} + W.\frac{dG}{dt} = (VRW) + (WRV)$$

$$+ (WGW) = 0$$

$$\therefore T = \text{constant.}$$

9. These three integrals however are not sufficient to determine the motion completely. We require three more scalar

9

(or one vector) integrals for determining the two vectors V and W. The difficulty of finding them is avoided in two cases :—

(i) When $R = 0$, in which case we can utilise the known solution of Poinsot in Rigid Dynamics.

(ii) Steady motion, when $\dfrac{dV|}{dt} = 0$ and $\dfrac{dW}{dt} = 0$, so that t is got rid of altogether from our equations of motion.

10. The case $R = 0$, is fully worked out in Lamb's Hydrodynamics, § 125. It may be interesting, just by the way, to put the solution in vector form.

The equations of motion reduce, when $R = 0$, to

$$\frac{dG}{dt} = G \times W.$$

Again, putting $R = 0$ in equations (3) p. 81,

we have $$V = -\phi_1^{-1}\phi_2 W,$$

$$G = -\phi'_2\phi_1^{-1}\phi_2 W + \phi_3 W.$$

Now ϕ_3 is self conjugate. Also, the conjugate of a 'product' of linear vector functions being the 'product' of their conjugates taken in the opposite order (Gibbs' Vector Analysis, Chap. V, p. 295), and further ϕ_1 and therefore ϕ_1^{-1} also being self conjugate, the conjugate of $\phi'_2\phi_1^{-1}\phi_2$ is itself. That is, G is a self conjugate linear vector function of W.

Hence, $G = \frac{1}{2} \nabla_w (G.W)$ [see p. 28.]

It follows that Poinsot's solution is applicable.

11. But the case of steady motion does not seem to have received yet the attention it deserves. Two simple particular cases are well known—the permanent translation and the permanent screws that we have when $R = 0$. It is proposed to have a general investigation of the question here.

If $\dfrac{dV}{dt}$ and $\dfrac{dW}{dt}$ are both zero, $\dfrac{dR}{dt} = 0$ and $\dfrac{dG}{dt} = 0$, and our equations of motion of page 82 reduce to

$$R \times W = 0$$
$$\text{and } R \times V + G \times W = 0$$ \quad (4)

The first equation shows that R is parallel to W, or $R = -vW$, where x is a scalar. Substituting in the second, we have

$$(xV + G) \times W = 0.$$

Again, putting $R = -xW$ in equations (3), p. 81, we have

$$V = -x\phi_1^{-1}W - \phi_1^{-1}\phi_2 W, \qquad (5)$$
$$\text{and } G = -x\phi'_2\phi_1^{-1}W - \phi'_2\phi_1^{-1}\phi_2 W + \phi_3 W.$$

Therefore, $-(xV + G) = x^2\theta_1 W + x\theta_2 W + \theta_3 W = \Omega W,$

where, $\theta_1 = \phi_1^{-1}$, $\theta_2 = \phi_1^{-1}\phi_2 + \phi'_2\phi_1^{-1}$, $\theta_3 = \phi'_2\phi_1^{-1}\phi_2 - \phi_3$,

and Ω has been written for the linear vector function

$$x^2\theta_1 + x\theta_2 + \theta_3.$$

We have, then, $\qquad \Omega W \times W = 0 ; \qquad (6)$

and our conclusion is that in any case of steady motion W should be parallel to ΩW.

12. By the rule for the conjugate of a product of linear vector functions quoted in § 10, we see immediately that $\theta_1, \theta_2, \theta_3$ and therefore Ω also are self conjugate linear vector functions.

We recall now Hamilton's theorem of the latent cubic of a linear vector functions.—In general, for any linear vector function ϕ, there are three vectors, say $\lambda_1, \lambda_2, \lambda_3$, of which the directions are left unaltered by the operation of that function. If g_1, g_2, g_3 are the roots of the cubic equation

$$g^3 - m''g^2 + m'g - m = 0,$$

where $m = \dfrac{\phi\alpha \cdot \phi\beta \times \phi\gamma}{\alpha \cdot \beta \times \gamma}$, $m' = \dfrac{\Sigma[\alpha \cdot \phi\beta \times \phi\gamma]}{\alpha \cdot \beta \times \gamma}$,

and $m'' = \dfrac{\Sigma[\beta \times \gamma . \phi\alpha]}{\alpha . \beta \times \gamma}$

a, β, γ being any three arbitrary non-coplanar vectors, then, $\phi\lambda_1 = g_1\lambda_1$, $\phi\lambda_2 = g_2\lambda_2$ and $\phi\lambda_3 = g_3\lambda_3$. The cubic in g is called the latent cubic of ϕ, and its roots the latent roots, and the vectors $\lambda_1, \lambda_2, \lambda_3$ which retain their old directions after the operation of ϕ are called the axes of ϕ. If ϕ is self conjugate, the latent roots are all real, and the three axes real and mutually perpendicular. [Killand and Tait's Quaternions, Chap X.].

Applying this theorem, we conclude that for any x there are three mutually perpendicular directions for W, corresponding to any one of which we may have a case of steady motion. Further, if y is the latent root of Ω corresponding to the axis W, $\Omega W = yW$, and we have $xV + G = -yW$, or $G = -xV - yW$.

Thus our impulse is given by

$$R = -xW \qquad \left.\begin{array}{l} \\ \\ \end{array}\right\} \qquad (7)$$
$$\text{and } G = -xV - yW.$$

13. To construct a screw, therefore, such that the corresponding motion of the solid may be steady, we find an axis of the linear vector function $\Omega(r)$ corresponding to any x and take W along this axis. V then is given by (5), p. 85 to be $-x\phi_1^{-1}W - \phi_1^{-1}\phi_2 W$. Draw the vector $\dfrac{W \times V}{W \cdot W}$ and through its extremity draw a line parallel to W. This line is the axis of the screw. If then the motion is started by the impulse $R = -xW$ and $G = -xV - yW$, the solid will continue to have the steady twist on our screw, the angular velocity being W and the pitch $\dfrac{W \cdot V}{W \cdot W}$.

It is easily seen the axis of any screw and the axis of the corresponding wrench coincide. For these axis being parallel to W and R respectively are themselves parallel. Further,

since, $\dfrac{R \times G}{R \cdot R} = \dfrac{-x\dot{W} \times (-xV - yW)}{(-xW).(-xW)} = \dfrac{W \times V}{W.W}$, these lines are drawn through the same point, so that the lines coincide and either line is fixed in space.

If p, p' denotes the pitches of the screw and wrench (R.G) respectively,

$$p' = \frac{R.G}{R.R} = \frac{-xW.(-xV-yW)}{(xW).(-xW)} = p + \frac{y}{x}$$

14. We conclude then that any x being specified, three mutually perpendicular (though not necessarily intersecting) screws of steady motion are determinate, except only as to the magnitude of W ; and again that, by varying r, the directions of screws of all possible steady motions would be obtained by solving the vector equation $\Omega(r) \times r = 0$, or $(x^2\theta_1 r + x\theta_2 r + \theta_3 r) \times r = 0$, in other words, by finding an axis of the linear vector function Ω.

It would be interesting now to enquire to what values of x correspond the two cases mentioned in § 11, $viz.$, permanent translation and steady motion with $R = 0$.

Since, in any case, $R = -xW$ and W is not supposed to be infinite, $R = 0$ would make $x = 0$. Ω now reduces to θ_3, $G = -yW = -\theta_3 W$, $V = -\phi_1^{-1}\phi_2 W$.

Since, again, when the motion of the solid is one of translation only, $W = 0$ and the screw reduces to V only; and since, in any case, R is supposed to be finite, we see that in this case x tends to infinity in such a manner that $xW = -R$. The equations (6) of p. 86, being written

$$(x\theta_1 W + \theta_2 W + \frac{1}{x}\theta_3 W) \times R = 0,$$

we see that in this case $\theta_1 R \times R = 0$, $i.e.$ $\phi_1^{-1}R \times R = 0$.

Hence the axis of the wrench, and therefore the axis of the screw also is parallel to r, where r satisfies $\phi_1^{-1}r \times r = 0$. That is, V is parallel to an axis of ϕ_1^{-1} or to an axis of ϕ_1, since ϕ_1 and ϕ_1^{-1} are co-axial.

These permanent translations, of course, could be worked out more directly by putting $W=0$ in (4) of p. 85 and (3) of p. 81.

15.   If we eliminate ι from

$$(\iota^2\theta_1 r + \iota\theta_2 r + \theta_3 r) \times \iota = 0,$$

we shall obtain the whole assemblage of lines, to one of which the axis of the screw corresponding to any case of steady motion must be parallel.

Multiplying scalarly by $\theta_1 r$ and $\theta_2 r$ respectively, we have

$$\iota\theta_1 r.\theta_2 r \times r + \theta_1 r.\theta_3 r \times r = 0,$$

and $\iota^2\theta_2 r.\theta_1 r \times r + \theta_2 r.\theta_3 r \times r = 0.$

$$\therefore \left[\frac{\theta_3 r.\theta_1 r \times r}{\theta_1 r.\theta_2 r \times r}\right]^2 = \frac{\theta_2 r.\theta_3 r \times r}{\theta_1 r.\theta_2 r \times r},$$

or, $(\theta_1 r.\theta_2 r \times r)\,(\theta_2 r.\theta_3 r \times r) = (\theta_3 r.\theta_1 r \times r)^2,$

which is homogeneous and of the sixth degree in the tensor of r, and represents therefore a cone of the sixth order, to some generator of which the axis of every steady screw must be parallel.

Obviously, the axes of the linear vector functions θ_1 and θ_3, —which we came across as giving the directions of screws for the special cases, § 14,—all lie on this cone, for the equation is identically satisfied if we put either $\theta_1 r \times r = 0$ or $\theta_3^r \times r = 0$.

16.   The motion of the solid being thus a twist about a screw of which the axis is fixed in space and pitch constant, it is almost obvious that each individual point of the solid would be describing a helix about the fixed axis of the screw and having the same pitch p (except of course points on the axis which would move along the axis).   For, if referred to a fixed origin O' on the axis, the position of any point P of the solid is specified by $r,(\overline{O'P}=r)$, the velocity of P is $\dfrac{dr}{dt}=pW+W \times r.$

Hence, $(W \times r).\dfrac{d}{dt}(W \times r) = W \times r. (W \times \dfrac{dr}{dt}) = W \times r.$

$$[W \times (W \times r)] = 0$$

which shows that $(W \times r).(W \times r)$ is constant, or the magnitude of $W \times r$ is constant. That is, the distance PN of P from the axis of W is constant.

The formula for $\dfrac{dr}{dt}$ shows, moreover, that the velocity parallel to W is pW, and velocity in plane perpendicular to W is $W \times r$, so that the motion in this plane is instantaneously in a circle (of which the centre is N and radius NP) with angular velocity $|W|$. Hence P moves in a helix of which the

pitch $= \dfrac{|pW|}{|W|} = p.$

17. For the maintenance of a motion of this type, appropriate forces must be continuously acting on the solid, for we know that the only motion a solid is capable of under no forces is either one of uniform translation, or a uniform translation combined with a motion of rotation about a principal axis of the solid at the centre of gravity. We shall just verify that fluid presssures exert on the solid just the force and couple necessary for the maintenance of the sort of motion that we have here.

Considering the general case (where the motion is not necessarily steady), let ξ', λ' denote the force and couple which the fluid pressures on the solid are equivalent to. The linear and angular moments of the solid are respectively

$$R_2 = m(V + W \times \bar{r}) \text{ and } G_2 = m\bar{r} \times V + \omega(W), \qquad . \quad (8)$$

these being just the terms of R and G that are obtained from T_2 by the operation of ∇_v and ∇_w respectively. For the solid alone, therefore, the equations of motion are

$$\frac{dR_2}{dt} = R_2 \times W + \xi'$$

and $$\frac{dG_2}{dt} = R_2 \times V + G_2 \times W + \lambda'.$$

If we further put now $R_1 = \int U da$ and $G_1 = \int U r \times da$, we have $R = R_1 + R_2$, $G = G_1 + G_2$. From our equations of motion therefore of p. 32, we have

$$\frac{dR_1}{dt} = R_1 \times W - \xi' \text{ and } \frac{dG_1}{dt} = R_1 \times V + G_1 \times W - \lambda'$$

Hence, $\xi' = -\dfrac{dR_1}{dt} + R_1 \times W$ and $\lambda' = -\dfrac{dG_1}{dt}$

$$+ R_1 \times V + G_1 \times W.$$

Considering steady motion now, for which $\dfrac{dR_1}{dt} = 0$ and

$\dfrac{dG_1}{dt} = 0$, we have

$$\xi' = R_1 \times W \text{ and } \lambda' = R_1 \times V + G_1 \times W,$$

or, using (4) p. 85.

$$\xi' = -R_2 \times W \text{ and } \lambda' = -R_2 \times V - G_2 \times W.$$

These formulae, for the special case of steady motion, could

of course be obtained directly by putting $\dfrac{dR_2}{dt} = 0$ and $\dfrac{dG_2}{dt} = 0$

in the equations of motion of the solid above.

Substituting now the values of R_2, G_2 given in (8), we obtain after slight reductions,

$$\xi' = W \times m(V + W \times \bar{r})$$

and $$\lambda' = m(V \times W) \times \bar{r} - \omega(W) \times W.$$

If, again, we refer the motion to the centre of gravity of the body as origin, so that $\bar{r}=0$, we have

$$\xi' = m\mathbf{W} \times \mathbf{V}$$

$$\text{and } \lambda' = \mathbf{W} \times \omega(\mathbf{W}), \qquad \right\} \qquad \qquad (9)$$

where $\omega(\mathbf{W})$ now is the angular momentum of the solid about its centre of gravity.

We notice that ξ' and λ' both vanish only if either (i) $\mathbf{W}=0$, or (ii) $\mathbf{V}$, $\mathbf{W}$ and $\omega(\mathbf{W})$ are collinear. The first is the case of one of the three permanent translations. In the second case, since $\mathbf{W}$ and $\omega(\mathbf{W})$ have the same direction, $\mathbf{W}$ is along an axis of the linear vector function ω, *i.e.*, along a principal axis of the solid at its centre of gravity. The axis of the screw therefore is a principal axis of the solid at its centre of gravity. These two, of course, are precisely the cases in which we expected *á priori* that ξ', λ' should vanish.

We show now that in the general case ξ', λ' of formula (9) are just the force and couple that would make the solid continue to have its screw motion represented by $\mathbf{V}$, $\mathbf{W}$ at the centre of gravity. Since the motion of the centre of gravity and the rotation of the solid about the axis $\mathbf{W}$ at its centre of gravity can be considered independently, we show that the velocity $\mathbf{V}$ of the C.G. is maintained by ξ', and then, regarding now the C.G. at rest, that the rotation $\mathbf{W}$ by itself is maintained by λ'; or, what comes to the same thing, that the mass-acceleration of the C.G. is equal to ξ' and that the rate of change of angular momentum about *c.s.* is equal to λ'.

For, if referred to a fixed origin O' on the fixed axis of the screw, the position of the C.G. is specified by r, then its velocity

$$\frac{dr}{dt} = \mathbf{V}$$

$$= p\mathbf{W} + \mathbf{W} \times r,$$

$$\frac{d\mathbf{V}}{dt} = \mathbf{W} \times \frac{dr}{dt} = \mathbf{W} \times \mathbf{V}, \because \frac{d\mathbf{W}}{dt} = 0, \frac{dp}{dt} = 0 ;$$

10

$$\therefore \; m\frac{d\mathrm{V}}{dt} = m\mathrm{W} \times \mathrm{V}, \text{ which is our } \xi'.$$

Again, the angular momentum of the solid about the C.G. is $\omega(\mathrm{W})$, and in calculating its rate of change we take the C.G., which is now supposed to be at rest, as our origin. Since the "origin system" [see Silberstein's foot note cited on p. 74] is fixed in the body and rotates with it with angular velocity W,

$$\text{the rate of change in question} = \frac{d\omega(\mathrm{W})}{dt} - \omega(\mathrm{W}) \times \mathrm{W}$$

$$= \mathrm{W} \times \omega(\mathrm{W}), \; \left[\because \; \frac{d\mathrm{W}}{dt} = 0 \right],$$

which is our λ'.

18. Having thus considered the general character of steady motion in the preceding articles 11-17, we would next turn our attention to the question of stability of these steady motions. Before considering this question, however, it would be convenient to summarise here a few propositions on the linear vector function which we shall presently have occasion to use. The more important ones are taken directly from Kelland and Tait's Quaternions, Chap. X.

(i) From the well-known relation

$$r(\alpha\beta\gamma) = (r\beta\gamma)\alpha + (r\gamma\alpha)\beta + (r\alpha\beta)\gamma,$$

it follows easily enough, — say, by writing $\phi(r)$ in the form

$\lambda r + a.rb + c \times r$ of page 24—that

$$(\alpha\beta\gamma)\phi(r) = (r\beta\gamma)\phi(\alpha) + (r\gamma\alpha)\phi(\beta) + (r\alpha\beta)\phi(\gamma).$$

Here α, β, γ are any three arbitrary non-coplanar vectors, and r any fourth vector, and ϕ denotes a linear vector function. $(\alpha\beta\gamma)$ etc. of course, as explained on p. 6 stand for $a.\beta \times \gamma$, etc.

(ii) For inverting the function $\phi(r)$ we have, if we denote the inverse function by ϕ^{-1},

$$m\phi^{-1}(\lambda \times \mu) = \phi'\lambda \times \phi'\mu,$$

where $m(\alpha\beta\gamma) = (\phi\alpha\phi\beta\phi\gamma)$, and λ, μ any two vectors.

If we introduce the function ψ by the definition,

$$\psi(\lambda \times \mu) = \phi'\lambda \times \phi'\mu,$$

we may write symbolically $m\phi^{-1} = \psi$.

(iii) For inverting $\phi r + gr$, or $(\phi+g)r$, where g is a constant scalar, we have

$$(m + m'g + m''g^2 + g^3)\,(\phi+g)^{-1}(\lambda \times \mu) = (\phi'+g)\lambda \times (\phi'+g)\mu$$
$$= (\psi + g\chi + g^2)\,(\lambda \times \mu),$$

where m, m', m'' have the values defined on p. 86, *viz.* $m(\alpha\beta\gamma) = (\phi\alpha\phi\beta\phi\gamma)$, $m'(\alpha\beta\gamma) = \Sigma(\alpha\phi\beta\phi\gamma)$, $m''(\alpha\beta\gamma) = \Sigma(\beta\gamma\phi\alpha)$, and the function χ is defined by

$$\chi(\lambda \times \mu) = \phi'\lambda \times \mu + \lambda \times \phi'\mu.$$

(iv) Integrating ϕr over the surface of a parallelopiped of which the edges are the vectors α,β,γ we get easily enough $\int \phi r.d\sigma = \Sigma(\beta\gamma\phi\alpha)$.

Hence our $m'' = \dfrac{\int \phi r.d\sigma}{(\alpha\beta\gamma)}$ =scalar constant of ϕ

(v) We have also for any vector λ.

$$m''\lambda = \phi\lambda + \chi\lambda,$$

or, symbollically, $m'' = \phi + \chi$.

(vi) We already enunciated Hamilton's theorem of the latent cubic on page 86. We only note here that if for any function ϕ, $m = 0$, the product of the three roots g_1, g_2 and g_3 of the latent cubic vanishes and therefore one of the roots, say g_1, is zero. It follows that for such a function there exists a vector λ_1 such that $\phi\lambda_1 = 0$. Conversely, if for a function ϕ we can find a vector λ_1 such that $\phi\lambda_1 = 0$, m for that function must vanish

Keeping to Gibbs' notation, we shall speak of m for any function ϕ as its *determinant* and denote it by $|\phi|$.

(vii) About the determinants of linear vector functions, we have the theorems that the determinant of a 'product' of linear vector functions is the product of their determinants, and that the determinant of the 'quotient' of two linear vector functions is the quotient of their determinants. Thus the determinant of $\phi_1\phi_2\phi_3^{-1} = \dfrac{|\phi_1|\,|\phi_2|}{|\phi_3|} = \dfrac{m_1 m_2}{m_3}$, if m_1, m_2, m_3 are the determinants of ϕ_1, ϕ_2, ϕ_3 respectively. [See Gibbs, p. 312.]

(viii) The inverse of the 'product' of any number of linear vector functions is the 'product' of their inverses taken in the opposite order. [Gibbs, p. 293]. Thus the inverse of $\phi_1\phi_2\phi_3 = (\phi_1\phi_2\phi_3)^{-1} = \phi_3^{-1}\phi_2^{-1}\phi_1^{-1}$.

19. To examine now the stability of any particular mode of steady motion, we consider as usual the effect of a small disturbance given to the system. V, W being the linear and angular velocities of the solid for the steady motion, and R, G the corresponding impulse, if δV, δW are the additional linear and angular velocities imparted to the solid by the disturbance, the total impulse that would generate from rest the new disturbed motion is represented by

$$R + \delta R = \phi_1(V + \delta V) + \phi_2(W + \delta W)$$

and $G + \delta G = \phi'_2(V + \delta V) + \phi_3(W + \delta W)$,

so that $\delta R = \phi_1(\delta V) + \phi_2(\delta W)$

and $\delta G = \phi'_2(\delta V) + \phi_3(\delta W)$.

Our equations of motion of p. 82 now are

$$\frac{d}{dt}(R + \delta R) = (R + \delta R) \times W + \delta W)$$

and $\dfrac{d}{dt}(G + \delta G) = (R + \delta R) \times (V + \delta V) + (G + \delta G) \times (W + \delta W)$, which, by the condition of steady motion [§ 11, p. 85], reduce to

$$\frac{d\delta R}{dt} = R \times \delta W + \delta R \times W,$$

$$\text{and } \frac{d\delta G}{dt} = (R \times \delta V + \delta R \times V + G \times \delta W + \delta G \times W,$$

if we neglect the terms $\delta R \times \delta W$, $\delta R \times \delta V$ and $\delta G \times \delta W$. Using (7) of p. 87, these equations further reduce to

$$\frac{d\delta R}{dt} = (\delta R + \delta W) \times W,$$

$$\text{and} \frac{d\delta G}{dt} = (\delta R + \delta W) \times V + (\delta G + \delta V + y\delta W) x W. \qquad \left.\right\} \quad (10)$$

20. Let us put now $\delta V = v e^{nt}$ and $\delta W = w e^{nt}$, where v, w are two vectors independent of t, so that

$$\delta R = R' e^{nt} \text{ and } \delta G = G' e^{nt},$$

$$\text{where} \quad R' = \phi_1 v + \phi_2 w$$
$$\text{and} \quad G' = \phi'_2 v + \phi_3 w \ ; \qquad \left.\right\} \qquad \quad . \ (11)$$

$$\text{and} \quad \frac{d\delta R}{dt} = n e^{nt} R', \ \frac{d\delta G}{dt} = n e^{nt} G'.$$

Equations (10) then are identically satisfied provided

$$n R' = (R' + w) \times W,$$
$$\text{and} \quad n G' = (R' + w) \times V + (G' + v + yw) \times W \ ; \qquad \left.\right\} \ \cdots \ (12)$$

$$\text{or,} \qquad \Phi_1 v + \Phi_2 w = 0,$$
$$\text{and} \quad \Phi_3 v + \Phi_4 w = 0 \ ; \qquad \left.\right\} \qquad \cdots \qquad \cdots \ (13)$$

$$\text{where} \ \Phi_1 v = n\phi_1 v - \phi_1 v \times W,$$
$$\Phi_2 w = n\phi_2 w - (\phi_2 + x)w \times W,$$
$$\Phi_3 v = n\phi'_2 v - \phi_1 v \times V - (\phi'_2 + x)v \times W,$$
$$\text{and} \quad \Phi_4 w = n\phi_3 w - (\phi_2 + x)w \times V - (\phi_3 + y)w \times W. \qquad \left.\right\} \ \cdots \ (14)$$

From (13) now we have $v = -\Phi_1^{-1}\Phi_2 w$ ... (15)

and $-\Phi_3\Phi_1^{-1}\Phi_2 w + \Phi_4 w = 0$ ... (16)

It follows that the latent cubic of the function $-\Phi_3\Phi_1^{-1}\Phi_2 + \Phi_4$ has a zero root and w is the corresponding axis. Thus the determinant of the function vanishes and we have

$$[\Phi_4 a - \Phi_3\Phi_1^{-1}\Phi_2 a] \cdot [\Phi_4 \beta - \Phi_3\Phi_1^{-1}\Phi_2 \beta] \times [\Phi_4 \gamma - \Phi_3\Phi_1^{-1}\Phi_2 \gamma] = 0,$$

[See (ii) and (vi), § 18]

a, β, γ being any set of three non-coplanar vectors ; that is,

$$\Phi_4 a . \Phi_4 \beta \times \Phi_4 \gamma - \Phi_3\Phi_1^{-1}\Phi_2 a . \Phi_3\Phi_1^{-1}\Phi_2 \beta \times \Phi_3\Phi_1^{-1}\Phi_2 \gamma$$

$$-\Sigma[\Phi_4 a \, \Phi_4 \beta \times \Phi_3\Phi_1^{-1}\Phi_2 \gamma] + \Sigma[\Phi_4 a . \Phi_3\Phi_1^{-1}\Phi_2 \beta \times \Phi_3\Phi_1^{-1}\Phi_2 \gamma] = 0.$$

Dividing out by $(a\beta\gamma)$, and noting that by § 18, (vii) p. 99, the

determinant of $\Phi_3\Phi_1^{-1}\Phi_2 = \dfrac{|\Phi_3| \; |\Phi_2|}{|\Phi_1|}$, we have

$$|\Phi_4| - \frac{|\Phi_3| \; |\Phi_2|}{|\Phi_1|} - \frac{1}{(a\beta\gamma)}\Sigma[\Phi_4 a . \Phi_4 \beta \times \Phi_3\Phi_1^{-1}\Phi_2 \gamma]$$

$$+ \frac{1}{(a\beta\gamma)}\Sigma[\Phi_4 a . \Phi_3\Phi_1^{-1}\Phi_2 \beta \times \Phi_3\Phi_1^{-1}\Phi_2 \gamma] = 0 \quad ... \quad (17)$$

This relation (17) gives us an equation for the appropriate values of n, and only when the roots are all imaginary, would the motion be stable.

21. *Summary of results to be proved.*—It is very tedious now to calculate all the co-efficients of the several powers of n in this equation, and even when these co-efficients are calculated, it is found impossible to come to any definite conclusion as to the conditions of stability. The solution of the problem with any degree of completeness was therefore given up as hopeless by this method, and there is no point going here over all the elaborate analysis for obtaining the full equation in n. What we propose to do is just to obtain a few special results which can be proved without much trouble. Thus we shall show, in the first instance, that in the most general case our equation

for n is of the seventh degree, and that the co-efficient of n^7 is determined solely by the nature of the solid and does not vanish, unless some special limitation is imposed on its shape, say, by way of symmetry. If will follow that, being of an odd degree, this equation must have at least one real root, and that in general therefore, for any arbitrary x, we shall not have any stable steady motion at all. We shall next show that for some special values of x, the term independent of n in our equation vanishes, and then neglecting the root $n=0,-$ of. which the effect is simply to add a constant vector each to the values of δV and δW, and which therefore does not affect the question of stability either way,—we shall have our equation reduced to one of the sixth degree; and since an equation of an even degree may have all its roots imaginary, it is possible now for the motion to be stable. Instead of groping about then for the stable screws among the infinite system of steady screws, we shall be sure of this one fact that if any stable screws are there, they would be found only among the group determined by those values of x which make the term independent of n vanish. It will be shown again that in general there are six such values of x, and our conclusion would be that in any case there cannot be more than 18 ($=6 \times 3$) stable steady screws. We shall show finally that $x=0$ is one of these six values of x, and we shall conclude by working out this case completely.

22. To obtain the degree in n of the left hand side of (17), let us first express R' in terms of w from the first of the equations (12) of page 101.

Writing $\phi R'$ for $nR' - R' \times W$ for the time being, this equation is $\phi R' \equiv nR' - R' \times W = xw \times W$. Hence by (ii) of § 18, p. 97, we have

$$mR' = xm\phi^{-1}(w \times W) = x\phi'w \times \phi'W,$$

where $\phi'w$ is the conjugate of ϕw and is therefore $nw + w \times W$ and $\phi'W = nW$, and

$$m(a\beta\gamma) = (na - a \times W).(n\beta - \beta \times W) \times (n\gamma - \gamma \times W),$$ which, again being written out in full, is easily found to be equal to $n^3(a\beta\gamma) + nW.W(a\beta\gamma)$, so that $m = n(n^2 + W.W)$.

Thus we have, $n(n^2 + \text{W.W})\text{R}' = x(nw + w \times \text{W}) \times n\text{W}$,

or, $\quad (n^2 + \text{W.W})\text{R}' = x[n(w \times \text{W}) + (w \times \text{W}) \times \text{W}]$

$$= x[n(w \times \text{W}) + \text{W}.w\text{W} - \text{W.W}w], \text{ p. 6,} \qquad \dots \ (18)$$

23. Now from (11) p. 101, $\text{R}' = \phi_1 v + \phi_2 w$. Therefore, $v = -\phi_1^{-1}\phi_2 w + \phi_1^{-1}\text{R}'$. Equating this value of v and the value in (15), p. 101, we have, by using (18),

$$-v = \Phi_1^{-1}\Phi_2 w = \phi^{-1}\phi_2 w - \frac{x}{n^2 + \text{W.W}} \ [n\phi_1^{-1}(w \times \text{W}) + \text{W}.w\phi_1^{-1}\text{W}$$

$$- \text{W.W}\phi_1^{-1}w]$$

$$= \frac{1}{n^2 + \text{W.W}} \ [n^2\phi_1^{-1}\phi_2 w - n.x\phi_1^{-1}(w \times \text{W})$$

$$+ \text{W.W}\phi_1^{-1}(\phi_2 + x)w - \text{W}.wx\phi_1^{-1}\text{W}]$$

Looking up the form of Φ_3 now in (14), p. 101, we see that we can write $\Phi_3\Phi_1^{-1}\Phi_2 w = \dfrac{1}{n^2 + \text{W.W}} \ [n^3\text{A} + n^2\text{B} + n\text{C} + \text{D}]w$, where A, B, C, D denote certain linear vector functions which do not involve n in their constitution. We have, for instance.

$$\text{A}w = \phi'_2\phi_1^{-1}\phi_2 w, \qquad \qquad . \ (19)$$

and again, it is easily seen also, that

$$-\text{D}w = \phi_1[\text{W.W}\phi_1^{-1}(\phi_2 + x)w - \text{W}.wx\phi_1^{-1}\text{W}] \times \text{V}$$

$$+ (\phi'_2 + x)[\text{W.W}\phi_1^{-1}(\phi_2 + x)w - \text{W}.wx\phi_1^{-1}\text{W}] \times \text{W}$$

$$= \text{W.W}[(\phi_2 + x)w \times \text{V} + (\phi'_2 + x)\phi_1^{-1}(\phi_2 + x)w \times \text{W}]$$

$$- x\text{W}.w[-\text{V} + (\phi'_2 + x)\phi_1^{-1}\text{W}] \times \text{W}$$

$$= \text{W.W}[(\phi_2 + x)w \times \text{V} + (\phi_3 + \Omega)w \times \text{W}]$$

$$- x\text{W}.w[2x\theta_1\text{W} + \theta_2\text{W}] \times \text{W}, \text{ by (5), p. 85,}$$

$$= \text{W.W}[(\phi_2 + x)w \times \text{V} + (\overline{\phi_3 + \Omega}\ w + \text{W}.w\text{F}) \times \text{W}], \quad \dots \ (20)$$

where Ω, θ_1, θ_2 are the linear vector functions defined on p. 86 and F has been written for the vector function of W,

$$- \frac{x}{\text{W.W}} \ [2x\theta_1\text{W} + \theta_2\text{W}].$$

24. Our $\Sigma[\Phi_4 a.\Phi_4 \beta \times \Phi_3 \Phi_1^{-1}\Phi_2 \gamma]$ of (17), p. 102, then, is of the form

$$\Sigma \frac{1}{n^2 + W.W} [(nA' + B')a.(nA' + B')\beta \times (n^3 A + n^2 B + nC + D)\gamma],$$

where $nA' + B'$ has been written for Φ_4, so that

$A'a = \phi_3 a$, and $-B'a = (\phi_2 + r)a \times V + (\phi_3 + y)a \times W$.

Obviously A', B' also do not involve n. We may write therefore

$$\frac{1}{(\alpha\beta\gamma)} \Sigma[\Phi_4 a.\Phi_4 \beta \times \Phi_3 \Phi_1^{-1}\Phi_2 \gamma]$$

$$\frac{1}{n^2 + W.W}[a_5 n^5 + a_4 n^4 + a_3 n^3 + a_2 n^2 + a_1 n + a_0]$$

where the a's are all independent of n. The values of a_5 and a_0 may be written down immediately. Thus

$$(\alpha\beta\gamma)a_5 = \Sigma[A'a.A'\beta \times A\gamma] = \Sigma[\phi_3 a.\phi_3 \beta \times \phi'_2 \phi_1^{-1}\phi_2 \gamma], \quad \cdots \quad (21)$$

and $\qquad\qquad (\alpha\beta\gamma)a_0 = \Sigma[B'a.B'\beta \times D\gamma] \qquad \cdots \quad (22)$

25. Again, with the same notation,

$$\frac{1}{(\alpha\beta\gamma)} \Sigma [\Phi_4 a. \Phi_3 \Phi_1^{-1}\Phi_2 \beta \times \Phi_3 \Phi_1^{-1}\Phi_2 \gamma]$$

$$= \frac{1}{(\alpha\beta\gamma)} \frac{1}{(n^2 + W.W)^2} \Sigma[(nA' + B')a. (n^3 A + n^2 B + nC + D)\beta$$

$$\times (n^3 A + n^2 B + nC + D)\gamma],$$

which is of form $\dfrac{1}{(n^2 + W.W)^2} [a'_7 n^7 + a'_6 n^6 + a_5 n^5 + ... + a'_0]$,

where also the co-efficients of the powers of n are independent of n. Clearly also,

$$(\alpha\beta\gamma)a'_7 = \Sigma[A'a. A\beta \times A\gamma] = \Sigma[\phi_3 a. \phi'_2 \phi_1^{-1}\phi_2 \beta$$

$$\times \phi'_2 \phi_1^{-1}\phi_2 \gamma], \quad \cdots \quad (23)$$

and $\qquad\qquad (\alpha\beta\gamma)a'_0 = \Sigma[B'a. D\beta \times D\gamma] \qquad\qquad . \quad (24)$

11

26.　We try to form an idea now of the other terms

$| \Phi_1 |$, $| \Phi_2 |$ and $| \Phi_3 |$ that occur in (17), p, 102.

(*i*) We note in the first instance that $\phi(r)$ being any liner vector function and a any constant vector, the determinant of $\phi r \times a$ vanishes. For,

$$(\phi a \times a).(\phi\beta \times a) \times (\phi\gamma \times a) = [\phi a \times a].\, a(\phi\beta\phi\gamma a) = 0, \text{ [page 6.]}$$

It follows that the parts independent of n in $\Phi_1^{\neg} r$ and $\Phi_2 r$, *viz.*, $-\phi_1 r \times W$ and $-(\phi_1 + x)r \times W$ have their determinants equal to zero.

(*ii*) We note again that if ϕ_1, ϕ_2 are any two linear vector functions, the determinant of $n\phi_1 r + \phi_2 r$ is easily found by writing out the expanded form of

$$\frac{1}{(a\beta\gamma)} \left[(n\phi_1 a + \phi_2 a).(n\phi_1\beta + \phi_2\beta) \times (n\phi_1\gamma + \phi_2\gamma) \right],$$

to be $m_1 n^3 + \mu n^2 + \mu' n + m_2$, where m_1, m_2 are the determinants of ϕ_1, ϕ_2 respectively and μ, μ' are determined from

$$\mu(a\beta\gamma) = \Sigma[\phi_1 a.\ \phi_1\beta \times \phi_2\gamma]$$

$$\text{and } \mu'(a\beta\gamma) = \Sigma[\phi_1 \acute{a}.\ \phi_2\beta \times \phi_2\gamma]$$

It follows that the terms independent of n vanish in both $| \Phi_1 |$ and $| \Phi_2 |$. We find, in fact, by working out

$$\frac{1}{(a\beta\gamma)} \left[(n\phi_1 a - \phi_1 a \times W).(n\phi_1\beta - \phi_1\beta \times W) \times (n\phi_1\gamma - \phi_1\gamma \times W) \right],$$

as in § 22, that

$$| \Phi_1 | = m_1 n(n^2 + W.W),$$

where m_1 is the determinant of ϕ_1.

We may write also

$$| \Phi_2 | = m_2 n^3 + b_2 n^2 + c_2 n,$$

$$| \Phi_3 | = m_2 n^3 + b_3 n^2 + c_3 n + d_3,$$

$$| \Phi_4 | = m_3 n^3 + b_4 n^2 + c_4 n + d_4,$$

where m_2 is the determinant of either of the two conjugate functions ϕ_2, ϕ'_2 and m_3 is the determinant of ϕ_3, and the b's, c's and d's are all independent of n and in general none of them vanishes.

27. For our equation in n then, corresponding to (17) p, 102, we have

$$m_2 n^3 + b_4 n^2 + c_4 n + d_4$$

$$-\frac{(m_3 n^3 + b_3 n^2 + c_3 n + d_3)(m_2 n^2 + b_2 n + c_2)}{m_1(n^2 + W.W)}$$

$$-\frac{a_5 n^5 + \ldots + a_0}{n^2 + W.W}$$

$$+\frac{a'_7 n^7 + \ldots + a'_0}{(n^2 + W.W)^2}$$

$$= 0. \qquad \ldots \qquad \ldots \qquad .. \qquad \ldots \quad (25)$$

Multiplying out by $(n^2 + W.W)^2$, we get an equation of the seventh degree in n.

The co-efficient of n^7

$$= m_3 - a_5 + a'_7 - \frac{m_2^2}{m_1}$$

$$= |\phi_3| - \frac{1}{(a\beta\gamma)} \Sigma[\phi_3 a.\, \phi_3 \beta \times \phi'_2 \phi_1^{-1}\phi_2 \gamma]$$

$$+ \frac{1}{(a\beta\gamma)} \Sigma[\phi_3 a.\, \phi'_2 \phi_1^{-1}\phi_2 \beta \times \phi'_2 \phi_1^{-1}\phi_2 \gamma]$$

$$- |\phi'_2 \phi_1^{-1}\phi_2|,$$

by (21) p. 106 and (23) p. 107, and (vii), p. 99.

Remembering now theorem (ii), § 26, we see that this co-efficient $= |\phi_3 - \phi'_2 \phi_1^{-1}\phi_2| = -|\theta_3|, \theta_3$ having the same definition as on p. 86. Obviously, our co-efficient of n^7 does not vanish, unless the functions ϕ_1, ϕ_2 and ϕ_3 are given in special ways, unless, that is to say, some special restriction is imposed on the shape of the moving solid, for these functions are solely determined by the form of the bounding surface of the solid.

28. We may write down also the term independent of n in the same equation. This term directly

$$=(W.W)^2 d_4 - a_o W.W + a'_o - W.W \frac{c_2 d_3}{m_1}$$

Now if, as in § 24, we write $n A' + B'$ for Φ_4, d_4 by (ii) § 26 is the determinant of B'. That is,

$$d_4(a\beta\gamma) = (B'aB'\beta B'\gamma).$$

The values of a_o, a'_o are given by (22) and (24), viz.,

$$(a\beta\gamma) \, a_o = \Sigma[B'a. \, B'\beta \times D\gamma] = W.W\Sigma[B'a.B'\beta \times D'\gamma],$$

$$(a\beta\gamma)a'_o = \Sigma[B'a. \, D\beta \times D\gamma] = (W.W)^2\Sigma[B'a. \, D'\beta \times D'\gamma],$$

if a new function D' is introduced by the definition

$$-D'r = \frac{1}{W.W} \, Dr, \text{ which by (20) p. 106}$$

$$\left. \begin{array}{c} =(\phi_2 + x)r \times V + [(\phi_3 + \Omega)r + W.rF] \times W, \\[2mm] \text{where} \quad F = -\frac{x}{W.W} \, [2x\theta_1 W + \theta_2 W] \end{array} \right\} \quad ...(26)$$

Hence, $(W.W)^2 d_4 - a_o W.W + a'_o$

$$=\frac{(W.W)^2}{(a\beta\gamma)} \, [(B'aB'\beta B'\gamma - \Sigma(B'aB'\beta D\gamma) + \Sigma(B'aD'\beta D'\gamma)]$$

$$=(W.W)^2[\mid B'-D' \mid + \mid D' \mid], \text{ by (ii), § 26,}$$

But $(B'-D')r = [(\Omega-y)r + W.rF] \times W,$

and, therefore, by (i) § 26, $\mid B'-D' \mid = 0.$

Therefore, $(W.W)^2 d_4 - a_o W.W + a'_o = (W.W)^2 \mid D' \mid .$

Hence our term independent of n

$$=W.W[W.W \mid D' \mid -\frac{c_2 d_3}{m_1}] = W.W[\mid D \mid -\frac{c_2 d_3}{m_1}] \quad ... \quad (27)$$

29. For further simplification of this term, we calculate generally the determinant of

$$\phi_1 \gamma \times V + \phi_2 \gamma \times W,$$

ϕ_1, ϕ_2 being any two linear vector functions.

Since the determinants of both $\phi_1 \gamma \times V$ and $\phi_2 \gamma \times W$ are zero by (i) § 26, the determinant in question is by (ii) § 26,

$$= \frac{1}{(\alpha\beta\gamma)} \left[\Sigma(\phi_1 \alpha \times V).\, (\phi_1 \beta \times V) \times (\phi_2 \gamma \times W) \right.$$

$$\left. + \Sigma(\phi_1 \alpha \times V).\, (\phi_2 \beta \times W) \times (\phi_2 \gamma \times W) \right]$$

Now $\Sigma(\phi_1 \alpha \times V) \times (\phi_1 \beta \times V).(\phi_2 \gamma \times W)$

$$= \Sigma(\phi_1 \alpha \phi_1 \beta V) V.\, (\phi_2 \gamma \times W)$$

$$= W \times V.\, \Sigma[(\phi_1 \alpha \phi_1 \beta V)\phi_2 \gamma]$$

$$= W \times V.\, \phi_2 \phi_1^{-1} V(\phi_1 \alpha \phi_1 \beta \phi_1 \gamma), \text{ by (i), § 18, p. 96}$$

$$= W \times V.\, \phi_2 \phi_1^{-1} V \, m_1(\alpha\beta\gamma), \, m_1 \text{ being } \; | \, \phi_1 \, | \, .$$

Again, $\Sigma(\phi_1 \alpha \times V).\, (\phi_2 \beta \times W) \times (\phi_2 \gamma \times W)$

$$= \Sigma(\phi_1 \alpha \times V).W(\phi_2 \alpha \phi_2 \gamma W)$$

$$= V \times W.\, \Sigma[(\phi_2 \beta \phi_2 \gamma W)\phi_1 \alpha]$$

$$= V \times W.\, \phi_1 \phi_2^{-1} W(\phi_2 \alpha \phi_2 \beta \phi_2 \gamma)$$

$$= V \times W.\, \phi_1 \phi_2^{-1} W \, m_2(\alpha\beta\gamma), \, m_2 \text{ being } \; ' \, \phi_2 \, |$$

The determinant of $\phi_1 r \times V + \phi_2 r \times W$ is therefore

$$= W \times V.\, [m_1 \phi_2 \phi_1^{-1} V - m_2 \phi_1 \phi_2^{-1} W] \qquad\qquad . \quad \text{(iii)}$$

$$= W \times V.\, [\phi_2 \psi_1 V - \phi_1 \psi_2 W], \text{ in the notation of (ii), p. 97}$$
$$\text{18.}$$

30. Applying this result now, we easily calculate d_3 and $| \, D' \, |$.

Thus, if we write $n\mathrm{A}'' + \mathrm{B}''$ for Φ_3, d_3 is by (ii), § 26 the determinant of B''. That is,

$$-d_3 = \text{determinant of } \phi_1 r \times \mathrm{V} + (\phi'_2 + x) r \times \mathrm{W}$$

$$= \mathrm{W} \times \mathrm{V}. \ [(\phi'_2 + x)\psi_1 \quad \mathrm{V} - \phi_1(\psi'_2 + x x_2 + x^2)\mathrm{W}], \text{ by}$$
(iii) § 18, p. 97

Again,$-|\ \mathrm{D}'\ | =$ determinant of $(\phi_2 + x) r \times \mathrm{V} + fr \times \mathrm{W}$,
[(26), p. 110]

if fr is written for the linear vector function $(\phi_3 + \Omega) r + \mathrm{W}.r\mathrm{F}$.

Hence, we have$-|\ \mathrm{D}'\ | = \mathrm{W} \times \mathrm{V}. \ [f(\psi_2 + x\, x_2 + x^2)\mathrm{V}$

$$-(\phi_2 + x)g\mathrm{W}],$$

where g denotes the ψ function for f, that is,

$$g\ (a \times \beta) = f'a \times f'\beta = [\phi_3 + \Omega)\ a + \mathrm{W}. \ \mathrm{F}a] \ \times \ [\phi_3 + \Omega)\ \beta$$

$$+ \mathrm{W}. \ \mathrm{F}\ \beta].$$

31. For the expression (27), c_2 only remains to be calculated. This is done directly. Thus by (ii), §. 26,

$$c_2\ (a\beta\gamma) = \Sigma\phi_2 a. \ [(\phi_2 + x)\ \beta \times \mathrm{W})] \times [(\phi_2 + x)\ \gamma \times \mathrm{W}]$$

$$= \Sigma\phi_2 a. \ \mathrm{W}\ [(\phi_2 + x)\ \beta \times (\phi_2 + x)\ \gamma. \ \mathrm{W}]$$

$$= \Sigma\phi_2 a. \ \mathrm{W}\ [(x^2 + x\chi'_2 + \psi'_2)\ \beta \times \gamma)]. \ \mathrm{W}, \ [\text{see } (iii), \text{ p. 97}]$$

$$= \Sigma\phi_2 a. \ \mathrm{W}\ [x^2\ (\beta\gamma\mathrm{W}) + x\ (\chi_2\mathrm{W}\beta\gamma) + (\psi_2\mathrm{W}\beta\gamma)]$$

$$= \mathrm{W}. \ [x^2\Sigma\ (\beta\gamma\mathrm{W})\ \phi_2 a + x\Sigma\ (x_2\mathrm{W}\beta\gamma)\phi_2\ a$$

$$+ \Sigma\ (\psi_2\mathrm{W}\beta\gamma)\ \phi_2 a]$$

which by (i), §18 $= (a\beta\gamma)\ \mathrm{W}. \ [x^2\phi_2\ \mathrm{W} + x\phi_2\chi_2\ \mathrm{W} + m_2\ \mathrm{W}]$,

since by (ii), §18, $\phi_2\psi_2\mathrm{W} = m_2\ \mathrm{W}$.

$$\therefore c_2 = x^2\ \mathrm{W}. \ \phi_2\ \mathrm{W} + x\ \mathrm{W}. \ \phi_2\chi_2\ \mathrm{W} + m_2\ \mathrm{W}. \ \mathrm{W}.$$

32. The term independent of n, then, in our equation for n is, as given in (27),

$$\mathrm{W}. \ \mathrm{W}\ \left[\mathrm{W}. \ \mathrm{W}\ |\ \mathrm{D}'\ | - \frac{c_2 d_3}{m_1}\right],$$

where c_2, d_3 and $\mid D' \mid$ have the values calculated in the last two articles. As explained in §21, it is necessary for stability that this term should vanish. A necessary, — of course, not sufficient — condition therefore that any one of the three steady screws corresponding to x should be stable, is that x should

satisfy $\qquad$ W. W $\mid$ D' $\mid - \dfrac{c_2 d_3}{m_1} = 0 \quad \ldots \qquad \qquad$. (28)

Since now x occurs in the first degree in V [(5), p. 85], in the second degree in Ω [p. 86] and F [(26), p. 110] and in the fourth degree in g, it appears from an inspection of the values of c_2, d_3 and $\mid D' \mid$ given in the last two articles, that (28) represents an equation of the sixth degree in x, and will, *in general*, therefore determine only six values of x. No x other than these six can possibly determine a stable steady screw.

33. We prove now that $x = 0$ is always one of this set of six values of x. It is only necessary to show that (28) is satis-fied when $x = 0$.

For, when $x = 0$, the expression for $-D'r$ in (26), p. 110 reduces to

$$\phi_2 r \times V + \phi'_2 \phi_1^{-1} \phi_2 r \times W,$$

F being zero, and $\phi_3 + \Omega$ reducing to $\phi_3 + \theta_3$, *i.e.* to $\phi'_2 \phi_1^{-1} \phi_2$ in this case. Hence now by (*iii*), p. 112,

$$- \mid D' \mid \; = W \times V . \, [m_2 \, \phi'_2 \phi_1^{-1} \phi_2 \phi_2^{-1} V - \mid \phi'_2 \phi_2^{-1} \phi_2 \mid$$
$$\phi_2 \, (\phi'_2 \phi_1^{-1} \phi_2)^{-1} W].$$

But, by (*vii*) and (*viii*), §18,

$$\mid \phi'_2 \phi_1^{-1} \phi_2 \mid \; = \frac{m_2^2}{m_1} \; \text{and} \; (\phi'_2 \phi_1^{-1} \phi_2)^{-1} = \phi_2^{-1} \phi_1 \phi'_2^{-1}.$$

Hence, $- \mid D' \mid \; = W \times V . \, [m_2 \phi'_2 \phi_1^{-1} V - \dfrac{m_2^2}{m_1} \, \phi_1 \phi'_2^{-1} W]$

$$= \frac{m_2}{m_1} \; W \times V . \, [\phi'_2 \psi_1 V - \phi_1 \psi'_2 W], \; \text{by (*ii*), §18.}$$

Also, putting $x=0$ in the values of c_2, d_3 in §§30, 31, we have now $c_2 = m_2$ W. W

and $-d_3 = $ W $\times$ V. $[\phi'_2 \; _1V - \phi_1 \psi'_2 W]$

It follows that W. W $\mid$ D$' \mid - \dfrac{c_2 d_3}{m_1} = 0$ identically when $x=0$.

34. Thus the case $x=0$ satisfies our necessary condition of stability. It is a relevant enquiry then if any one of three screws corresponding to this case is stable. This is the case (§14) when the impulse producing the original steady motion reduces to a couple alone, G $= -\theta_3$ W $= -y$W; R$=0$.

For equations (12) of p. 101, we write now

$$n R' = R' \times W$$

$$n G' = R' \times V + (G' + yw) \times W.$$

From the first, $R'=0$ (for no vector can be perpendicular to itself), and therefore the second reduces to

$$n G' = (G' + yw) \times W \qquad . \quad (29)$$

Putting again $R'=0$ in (11) p. 101, we have

$v = -\phi_1^{-1}\phi_2 w$, G$' = -\phi'_2\phi_1^{-1}\phi_2 w + \phi_3 w = -\theta_3 w$.

Writing ϕ for θ_3 for convenience, we have G$' = -\phi w$

and $\qquad \therefore \quad -n\phi w - (-\phi + y)\, w \times$ W $= 0$

or $\qquad n\phi w - (\phi - y)w \times$ W $= 0.$ $\qquad . \quad (30)$

Putting the determinant of the function on the left hand side of (30) to zero, we shall have our equation for the appropriate values of n in this case.

The determinant in question is, by (ii) § 26

$$m \; n^3 + bn^2 + cn + d.$$

where, $-d=$ determinant of $(-y)$ $w \times W = 0$, by (i) § 26 ;

$m =$ determinant of $\phi = |{}_3|$;

$c = y^2 W$. $\phi W - yW$. $\phi \chi W + mW$. W, just as in the calculation of c_2 in § 31 ;

and $-b\ (a\beta\gamma) = \Sigma(\phi a \times \phi \beta)$. $[\phi - y)\ \gamma \times W]$, which we find to be zero when we write it out and remember also that ϕ is self conjugate ; so that $b = 0$.

Hence, our equation for n now is

$$m\ n^3 + n\ [y^2 W.\ \phi W - yW.\ \phi \chi W + mW.\ W] = 0 \quad \ldots \ (31)$$

[We may note, by the way, here that the co-efficient of n^3 in this equation, *viz.*, m or $|{}_3|$, is the same (but for the sign) as the co-efficient of n^7 in the equation for n in the general case (see § 27, p. 109). Since this last co-efficient in any case is independent of x, and since equation (31) is only the reduced form, when $x = 0$, of the general seventh degree equation, we see that when $x = 0$, not only does the term independent of n vanish in the general equation, (as we have proved in § 33), but the co-efficients of all terms from n^4 downwards vanish too].

35. Now one root of equation (31) is $n = 0$, and the other two are given by

$$n^2 = -\ \frac{1}{m}\ [y^2 W.\ \phi W - yW.\ \phi \chi W + mW.\ W]$$

since $\phi W = yW$, and by (V) § 18, $\chi = m'' - \phi$, this simplifies to

$$n^2 = -\ \frac{W.\ W}{m}\ [2y^3 - m''y^2 + n].$$

The motion is stable, therefore, if y is so chosen that

$$\frac{1}{m}\ [2y^3 - m''y^2 + m] \quad \ldots \qquad \qquad . \ (32)$$

is positive. Now, by Hamilton's theorem of the latent cubic, (§ 12, p. 86) y may have any one of three values, *viz.*, the roots, say y_1, y_2, y_3, of the equation

$$y^3 - m''y^2 + m'y - m = 0,$$

so that $m'' = y_1 + y_2 + y^3, m' = y_2 y_3 + y_3 y_1 + y_1 y_2$ and $m = y_1 y_2 y_3$.
Putting, then, y equal to any one of these roots, say y_1,
expression (32) becomes

$$\frac{1}{y_1 \, y_2 \, y_3} \; [2y_1^3 - y_1^2 \, (y_1 + y_2 + y_3) \cdot y_1 y_2 y_3],$$

i.e. $\dfrac{1}{y_2 \, y_3} \; [y_1^2 - y_1 \, (y_2 + y_3) + y \bar{2} \, y_3],$

i.e. $\dfrac{1}{y_2 \, y_3} \; (y_1 - y_2) \, (y_1 - y_3) \; \cdots$. (33)

The steady screw, therefore, parallel to that axis of ϕ which
corresponds to the latent root y_1 is stable, if the expression (33)
is positive.

Since, R being zero, the energy of the steady motion for
any y is $\frac{1}{2}$ G. W $= - \frac{1}{2} y$ W. W, which must in any case be
positive, it follows that all the y's are negative. The expression
(33) therefore is positive, if y_1 is numerically either the greatest
or the least of the three numbers y_1, y_2, y_3, and it is negative,
if y_1 is intermediate in magnitude between y_2 and y_3. In this
last case, therefore, the motion is unstable, and it is stable in
either of the two other cases.

We may put the conclusion in another form. Since $-r.\phi r$
is always positive, $-r.\phi r = k$, where k is a positive constant
represents an ellipsoid, of which the principal axes are in the
directions of the axes of the linear vector function ϕ, and the
magnitudes of these principal axes are inversely proportional to
$\sqrt{-y_1}, \sqrt{-y_2}$ and $\sqrt{-y_3}$. Hence, the two steady motions
for which the screws are parallel to the greatest and least axes
of this ellipsoid are stable, and that steady motion for which
the screw is parallel to the mean axis is unstable.

Made in the USA
Monee, IL
07 July 2026

56551422R00059